George Sewall Boutwell

The lawyer, the statesman and the soldier

George Sewall Boutwell

The lawyer, the statesman and the soldier

ISBN/EAN: 9783337135379

Printed in Europe, USA, Canada, Australia, Japan

Cover: Foto ©Raphael Reischuk / pixelio.de

More available books at **www.hansebooks.com**

THE LAWYER

THE STATESMAN AND

THE SOLDIER

BY

GEORGE S. BOUTWELL

We value a man by the measure of his
strength at the place where he is strongest.

.

NEW YORK
D. APPLETON AND COMPANY
1887

INTRODUCTION.

THE preparation of these sketches is due to the circumstance that it is my fortune to have had the acquaintance of the persons to whom the sketches relate. These pages may show the marks of friendship rather than the skill of the biographer or the research of the historian. I have written in obedience to the rule or maxim that we value a man by the measure of his strength at the place where he is strongest. Human errors and weaknesses, from which none of us are exempt, can not be set off properly against great thoughts expressed or great acts performed. Errors and weaknesses mar the man, but they can not qualify the greatness achieved.

CONTENTS.

THE LAWYER, THE STATESMAN, AND THE SOLDIER.

RUFUS CHOATE.

IF in imagination we can command the presence of a man only less than six feet in height, with a full, deep breast, high and unseemly shoulders, hips and legs slender and in appearance weak, arms long, hands and feet large and ill-formed, a head broad, chaste, symmetrical, covered with a luxuriant suit of black, glossy, wavy hair, a face intellectually handsome and equally attractive to men and to women, a complexion dark and bronzed as becomes the natives of the tropical isles of the East, a beard scanty and vagrant, mouth and nose large, lips thin and long, an eye black, gentle and winning in repose, but brilliant, commanding, and persuasive in moments of excitement—we shall have thus and now created an imperfect picture of Rufus Choate as he presented himself to his contemporaries when his physical qualities had not been wasted by disease nor impaired by age.

And if from this sketch we are in doubt whether

the subject of it was an attractive person, we should realize that his manners and ways were as gentle as the manners and ways of the best bred woman, that to the young he was always kind and often affectionate, to the aged respectful, and that to those in authority he was ever deferential without being or appearing to be a sycophant.

And to these charms of person and benignity of manners we are to superadd a voice that in conversation, debate, or oration was copious, commanding, sonorous, and emotional, responding like music to every change of thought, and, in its variety of tone and sweep of accent and emphasis, touching and influencing not only the sentiments and feelings but even the opinions and judgments of men. His vocabulary knew no limits except those set by the language itself; and such was his facility in its use as to extort from the stern Chief-Justice of the Supreme Judicial Court of Massachusetts the remark, when told that Webster's new dictionary contained many thousand additional words, " I beg of you not to let Choate hear of it ! "

His gestures seemed extravagant often, but they were justified usually by the wonderful rhetoric which he commanded and so used that it was accepted as the natural, the inevitable outflow of his mind. While he seldom made a plain statement of the exact truth either in conversation or in argument, he yet expressed the truth by a manifest exaggeration of the truth.

When he offered wine to friends and omitted to join them, he said, "I keep a little wine in my house, but as for myself I don't drink a glass once in a thousand years." Borrowing the language of the profession in regard to challenges of jurors, he said of a brother at the bar whose manners and ways were disagreeable, "Some persons we hate for cause, but * * * we hate peremptorily."

Upon his return from the Senate of the United States in 1842, standing in the doorway of a meeting-house then nearly a century old in a country town of Massachusetts, and speaking to the multitude within and without the building, in explanation and defense of the bankrupt law then recently enacted under the lead of the Whig party, he emphasized and made attractive the restoration to active business of the body of bankrupts by the exclamation, "In an instant we created five hundred thousand full-grown, able-bodied men!"

Mr. Choate's facility in the use of language, his urbanity of manner, and his ability to express contempt without wounding visibly the subject of it, were illustrated when he was closing an argument in behalf of a client who was seeking compensation for injury to his person, his horse, carriage, and harness. Mr. Choate discoursed of the injury to his client, to the horse, and to the carriage, and was about taking his seat, when his junior touched him and said, "You have omitted the harness." Though annoyed by the suggestion of so insignificant a matter, he turned to the jury and with his accustomed urbanity, said—"Ah, Mr. Foreman and gentlemen of the jury, the harness!—a safe, sound, substantial, serviceable (pausing and dropping his voice), second-hand harness," and sat down.

Mr. Choate lived and labored under the influence of that dainty and dangerous gift of nature which finds relief only in physical excesses or in unremitting intellectual work—a sensitive, nervous organization. He seldom indulged himself in amusements and except when compelled by illness he had no relaxation from the toils of public and professional life.

When warned by an associate that his constant labors were imperiling his health, he said, " I have no alternative but the insane asylum."

Again, when asked how his constitution held out, he answered: "That was gone long ago; I am now living on the by-laws."

In Mr. Choate's nature there was a singular mixture of timidity and professional courage. It is said that in consultation with his associates he was too often doubtful of success, but, when the excitement of the trial was on, there were no indications of fear. His movements, tones, and arguments were those of an advocate accustomed to victory, and confident alike in his cause and in the supremacy of his own powers. But his constitutional timidity appeared in his politics and in his political career. It was unfortunately conspicuous in his controversy in the Senate with Mr. Clay, and in his acceptance in 1856 of the candidacy of Mr. Buchanan, manifestly through fear of a rupture with the South. It can not be denied, however, that his speech at Lowell in that year is full of statesmanship mingled with solemn prophecies as to the consequences of the slavery agitation, if only we accept his thesis that it was better to endure slavery than to suffer the horrors of civil war. In his opinion then, we had only a choice of evils. He chose to endure those we had, rather than to fly to others he knew not of. Genius in oratory and capacity in statesmanship are not often combined in the same person.

Nor can it be asserted with confidence that any great orator was ever eminently successful in the practicaal ffairs of government.

Cicero may have been an exception, but even his career is open to question in that respect. Certainly the elder Pitt, Burke, Lamartine, Kossuth, and Castelar are instances of failure, and some of them are conspicuous examples.

There is a rough side to government, and there must be a quality of harshness in the nature of those who administer governments successfully.

Mr. Choate's courtesy was unfailing. He submitted deferentially to the verdicts of juries and to the opinions of the bench. He avoided personal controversy with his brethren at the bar, and he treated witnesses upon the stand, whether friendly or hostile, with apparent kindly consideration. It was only in argument that witnesses felt the force and weight of his keen satire and persuasive logic. His presence of mind never failed, and his ready resources in the contests of the bar were not less remarkable than the brilliancy of his arguments.

Perhaps no advocate ever received a heavier blow from a witness than fell upon Mr. Choate when managing the defense of a shipmaster who was charged with the crime of robbing and sinking his vessel in the waters of the Indian Ocean. The mate had become a witness for the Government. Robert Rantoul, Jr., was the prosecuting district attorney. The mate was a party to the crime, and it was the theory of his testimony to prove that the captain originated the scheme, and that the mate and his associates were persuaded by the captain to engage in the undertaking. In the cross-examination Mr. Choate sought for the inducements and representations to which the mate had yielded.

The answers of the mate were reluctantly given, and he evidently held something back. At last Mr. Choate laid his elbows upon the table, rested his head upon his hands, and with a persuasive manner and voice said, "Now, my good fellow, will you not tell us what the captain said that induced you to engage in this business?" The witness replied with nervous impetuosity, and said, " He told us there was a man in Boston named Choate who would get us clear, if the money were found in our boots!" When the laughter and excitement had subsided, Mr. Choate, without change of voice or manner, said, " Did my brother Rantoul tell you to say that?" The witness, for a moment, was confounded by the address and personality of the question, and after some delay said, " No." Mr. Choate remarked, " We all knew he didn't, but why did you hesitate about that, as you have about everything you have told us to-day?" The rencontre left a wound on Mr. Choate, but the mode of escape was as good as the circumstances of the case permitted.

This incident in his career, and his successful defense of Albert J. Tirrell for the murder of Maria Bickford, were the basis of the keen and almost cruel attack made by Wendell Phillips, in his oration called " The Boston Idols."

The idols were Webster, Everett, and Choate.

In approaching Choate, he erected a pantheon, in which he put many of the great gods of jurisprudence, and accompanied their names with stately encomiums.

Among these were D'Agesseau, Romilly, and Mansfield. " Finally," said the orator, " New England shrieks, ' Here is Choate, who made it safe to murder, and for whose health thieves asked before they began to steal !' "

No greater tribute than this could be offered, either by friendly or hostile voice, to the learning, skill, and genius of an advocate ; but beneath the spoken word there lurks the suggestion that there are human powers so exalted and controlling that they ought not to be employed in defense of persons charged with crime.

All crimes are primarily against the Government, whatever may be the personal circumstances attending their commission.

The sufferers can in no case be their own avengers. In the pursuit and prosecution of criminals the resources of a state or of a nation are at the command of the agents of the Government. Those resources are always greater than the resources of the most opulent individual. The Government enacts the laws, creates the courts, ordains the mode of procedure, furnishes the juries from its body of citizens; and, since the employment of Mr.

Webster to aid the Attorney-General of Massachusetts in the prosecution of the Knapps for the murder of Joseph White, it has been thought not improper for Governments to retain eminent counsel
and advocates to aid or even to lead in the trial
of persons charged with crime. The advantages
could not be greater if it were the maxim of Governments that, for every crime committed, some
person should suffer a penalty. The ancient and
wiser maxim, that it is better that ninety-nine
guilty persons should escape than that one innocent person should suffer, assumes that it is a
higher duty to protect the innocent than to punish
the guilty. And this duty always rests upon the
Government

It is, therefore, a wise public policy which pro-
vides the means of defense for every person charged
with crime; and a healthy public sentiment will in
the end not only tolerate but it will support the advocate who undertakes the defense, even though
the accused for the moment may be enduring the
weight of an adverse and intolerant public judgment.

It is a public misfortune, whose effects run with
the ages, when great criminals even are brought to
the bar and tried and condemned without the support and aid of an able, vigorous, and persistent
defense. And it should ever be borne in mind that,

in cases where the guilt of the party is beyond
question, he is entitled to the benefit of every defense which the law authorizes ; and it should also
be borne in mind that, if those means are denied to
the guilty, the time will soon come when they will
not be a shield to the innocent.

The line of professional duty is clear. The attorney is an officer of the court. He is to obey the
law, and in his advice to clients he is always to direct them in the line of obedience to the law. Otherwise, he becomes a participator in their guilt.
Usually, however, the attorney is not consulted until the law has been violated. The accused is then
entitled to every advantage and privilege which
the law allows. These the attorney and advocate
are to find and to employ with whatever of ability
they can command, and if in the end the accused is found not guilty, the law presumes him
innocent; but, whether so or not, the fault, if
fault there be, is with the Government and its
agents.

Lord Brougham, in his defense of Queen Caroline, went much further. He maintained the extreme, revolutionary doctrine that it was the duty
of counsel to pursue the defense of clients even to
the destruction of the Government itself. This position, however, he qualified subsequently by declaring that he assumed it as a menace to the king,

and for the purpose of staying the hand of the prosecutors.

Mr. Choate's successful defense of Albert J. Tirrell was followed by severe criticisms, and the loss of public esteem among those whose narrow ethics could not comprehend the true relations of the Government to the individual members of society. Tirrell was a young man of irregular ways of life, and Maria Bickford was a young woman of great beauty and some celebrity. That Tirrell was her slayer there was no doubt. The defense was somnambulism on the part of Tirrell, and the habit was proved upon the testimony of his family and associates. The defense relied also on the absence of motive on the part of Tirrell.

Beyond this the witnesses for the Government, who had knowledge of the facts occurring during the night of the murder, and in the house where the killing took place, were persons of ill repute. The jury found the prisoner not guilty. The public found him guilty, and the public made Mr. Choate responsible for the verdict of the jury. When Mr. Choate declined the defense of Professor Webster, charged with the murder of Dr. Parkman, his course was attributed to his disinclination to again encounter the popular odium. It is more probable, however, that Mr. Choate declined the defense because Professor Webster

2

was unwilling to rely upon the actual facts, and
on which his crime would have been reduced
from murder to manslaughter.

Although Mr. Choate was destitute of many
of the qualities of statesmanship, his views of
public questions were those of a statesman. He
was conservative in his opinions, a follower of
Hamilton, and an associate and friend of Webster. If the Constitution of the country had been
the work of his own hand, his devotion to it
could not have been greater; but he was terrified
by the thought that it was a band of iron which
might be broken but could never be changed.
The civil war, which he dreaded, but lived not to
see, wrought changes in the Constitution that he
would have welcomed.

Mr. Choate's last public service was in the Constitutional Convention of Massachusetts of 1853.
In those days, in Massachusetts, we were blessed
with an excellent sergeant-at-arms, who, through
the agency of a boy blindfolded—a clairvoyant, no
doubt—was able usually to so draw the numbers
from a box as to secure a good seat for the leading
men of all parties. Mr. Choate drew an end-seat,
and it was my fortune to secure the next end-seat
immediately behind him. For about three months
we were thus associated. I enjoyed his conversation, observed his ways, and listened to

his speeches, which were, in fact, always orations.

During the months of May, June, and July, Mr.
Choate attended to some professional business, prepared and delivered his Dartmouth eulogy upon
Mr. Webster, and participated in the debates of the
convention. Worthy of especial notice were his
speeches upon the judiciary and the representative
system. The speech on the judiciary was delivered on a hot day in July. During all his mature
years Mr. Choate was subject to severe headaches,
and they often followed or attended the excitement
of public efforts. That day he provided himself
with a bottle of bay-rum, with which he bathed his
head frequently and profusely. His gesticulations
were so vigorous that drops of bay-rum and per-
spiration were thrown from his hair and bespat-
tered his neighbors. His speeches were usually
written, if the characters he employed could be
called writing, inasmuch as they were illegible to
every one but himself. In the delivery, however,
he dealt only with the sheets which he took up and
held, and laid down in succession, without appearing to read what was written. Probably a word
suggested an entire sentence or even a paragraph,
and thereupon his memory was quickened or his
mind repeated the process of thought pursued
when the sentence or paragraph was written.

When engaged in the trial of causes he usually
ran two sets of notes. Upon one he minuted questions or topics to be used in the cross-examination
of witnesses, and upon the other he noted points or
illustrations for his argument to the jury.

Neither eloquence nor argument is exclusively
of the word spoken. The tones, the gestures, the
emphasis, the accent, reveal the finer shades of
meaning on the one side and enforce the argument
on the other. Therefore, we can institute no comparison between the orators that we have heard
and the orators that we have not heard. In justice
we can only compare with one another the orators
that we have heard, and with one another the
orators that we have not heard.

Mr. Choate was a student in the office of William Wirt, and for a year he was a listener to the
arguments of William Pinckney in the Supreme
Court of the United States. On those models he
fashioned his career as an advocate, and on those
models he so improved, I imagine, as, in the end,
to defy rivalry and even comparison. But Mr.
Choate's laurels were gathered in a field where
there were many competitors both at the bar and
upon the rostrum. His antagonists and competitors were Webster, Mason, Franklin Dexter, Hil-
lard, Dana, Everett, Phillips, and, whether at the
bar or upon the platform, he could have com-

manded an audience at the expense of each and all
of those gifted men.

To these I may add, out of my own personal
experience, the names of Henry Clay, J. McPher-
son Berrien, Thomas Corwin, Abraham Lincoln,
George Thompson, Louis Kossuth, as persons
quite unequal to contest with Rufus Choate for
supremacy in ability to interest, instruct, and control a popular assembly,

Of Mr. Choate it is to be said that his philosophy and his powers of imagination passed not beyond the relations of men to men, and of men to
things. Hence, we shall seek in vain for idealistic
passages in his speeches and writings. We shall
find nothing that can be compared with Webster's
great passage in his eulogy on Jefferson and
Adams:

"A superior and commanding human intellect,
when Heaven vouchsafes so rare a gift, is not a
temporary flame burning brightly for a while and
then expiring, giving place to returning darkness;
it is rather a spark of fervent heat as well as a radi-
ant light, with power to enkindle the common mass
of human mind, so that when it glimmers in its
own decay, and finally goes out in death, no night
follows, but it leaves the world all light, all on fire,
from the potent contact of its own spirit."

Nor any passage which can be compared to
Buckle's tribute to men of thought and science:

" The discoveries of great men never leave us.
They are immortal. They contain those eternal
truths that survive the shock of empires, outlive
the struggles of rival creeds, and witness the decay
of successive religions. All these have their different standards and their different measures—one
set of opinions for one age and another set for another. They pass away like a dream. They are
as the fabric of a vision which leaves not a rack
behind. The discoveries of genius alone remain.
To them we owe all that we now have. They are
for all ages and all times. Never young and never
old, they bear the seeds of their own life. They
flow on in a perennial and undying stream. They
are essentially cumulative, and, giving birth to the
additions which they subsequently receive, they
thus influence the most distant posterity, and after
the lapse of centuries produce more effect than
they could do even at the moment of their promul-
gation."

It is a fortunate fact in the intellectual world
that the varieties of taste, power, and genius are so
many and distinguishing that comparisons elude us,
while contrasts are obvious to the most careless
observers. Mr. Choate combined a rare subtilty of
observation and ingenuity of argument, gilded by
an affluent imagination found nowhere else but in
the fields of romance, with a clear and incisive logic
which charmed alike the rustic and the student, and
compelled the assent of the critic and the judge.

If it be admitted that Mr. Choate has left no single passage that can be quoted by the side of the choice extracts from ancient and modern orations, it may nevertheless be claimed for him that his arguments and speeches are well sustained from first to last, and that the marks of rewriting and pruning are nowhere to be found. Such were his intellectual resources and such his mastery over his faculties that what he wrought was finished as he wrought.

Therefore, whatever selections we may make from the speeches and orations of his maturer years will express his quality and power, remembering always that the effect of his personal appearance, gestures, and electrical voice can never be comprehended by those who had not the fortune to see and to hear him.

In the Convention of 1853 a vigorous effort was made to change the tenure of the judicial office from a tenure of "good behavior" to a term of years. This change Mr. Choate resisted, and the speech he then delivered presents him at his best in the field of statesmanship.

His purpose he thus sets forth :

" I go for that system, if I can find it or help to find it, which gives me the highest degree of assurance, taking man as he is, at his strongest and at his weakest, and in the average of the lot of hu-

manity, that there shall be the best judge on every
bench of justice in the Commonwealth, through its
successive generations."

In a speech of two hours' duration he dealt
with the problem how to command and how to
keep upon the bench such a judge as he thus described :

"In the first place, he should be profoundly
learned in all the learning of the law, and he must
know how to use that learning. Will any one stand
up here to deny this? In this day, boastful, glori-
ous for its advancing, popular, professional, scientific, and all education, will any one disgrace himself
by doubting the necessity of deep and continued
studies, and various and thorough attainments to
the bench? He is to know not merely the law which
you make, and the Legislature makes, not constitutional and statute law alone, but that other ampler,
that boundless jurisprudence, the common law,
which the successive generations of the State have
silently built up ; that old code of freedom which
we brought with us in the Mayflower and Ara-
bella, but which, in the progress of centuries, we
have ameliorated and enriched, and adapted wisely
to the necessities of a busy, prosperous, and wealthy
community—that he must know.

"And where to find it? In volumes which you
must count by hundreds, by thousands ; filling
libraries; exacting long labors—the labors of a
lifetime, abstracted from business, from politics;

but assisted by taking part in an active judicial
administration ; such labors as produced the wisdom and won the fame of Parsons, and Marshall,
and Kent, and Story, and Holt, and Mansfield. If
your system of appointment and tenure does not
present a motive, a help for such labors and such
learning, if it discourages, if it disparages them, in
so far it is a failure.

" In the next place, he must be a man not
merely upright ; not merely honest and well-inten-
tioned—this of course—but a man who will not
respect persons in judgment. And does not every
one here agree to this also ? Dismissing for a moment all theories about the mode of appointing
him, or the time for which he shall hold office, sure
I am we all demand that, as far as human virtue,
assisted by the best contrivances of human wisdom, can attain to it, he shall not respect persons in
judgment. He shall know nothing about the parties, everything about the case. He shall do everything for justice, nothing for himself ; nothing for
his friend, nothing for his patrons, nothing for his
sovereign.

" If, on one side, is the executive power and the
Legislature and the people—the sources of his honors, the givers of his daily bread—and on the other
an individual, nameless and odious, his eye is to see
neither great nor small, attending only to the trepi-
dations of the balance. If a law is passed by a
unanimous Legislature, clamored for by the general
voice of the public, and a cause is before him on it,
in which the whole community is on one side and

an individual nameless or odious on the other, and
he believes it to be against the Constitution, he
must so declare it, or there is no judge. If Athens
comes there to demand that the cup of hemlock be
put to the lips of the wisest of men, and he believes
that he has *not corrupted the youth, nor omitted to worship the gods of the city, nor introduced new divinities
of his own*, he must deliver him, although the thun-
der light on the unterrified brow.

"And, finally, he must possess the perfect confidence of the community, that he bear not the sword
in vain. To be honest, to be no respecter of persons, is not yet enough. He must be believed
such. I should be glad so far to indulge an old-
fashioned and cherished professional sentiment as
to say that I would have something venerable and
illustrious attach to his character and function, in
the judgment and feelings of the Commonwealth.

"But if this should be thought a little above or
behind the time, I do not fear that I subject myself
to the ridicule of any one when I claim that he be
a man toward whom the love and trust and affectionate admiration of the people should flow; not a man
perching for a winter and summer in our court-
houses and then gone forever; but one to whose
benevolent face, and bland and dignified manners,
and firm administration of the whole learning of
the law, we become accustomed; whom our eyes
anxiously, not in vain, explore when we enter the
temple of justice; toward whom our attachment
and trust grow ever with the growth of his own
reputation: I would have him one who might look

back from the venerable last years of Mansfield or
Marshall and recall such testimonies as these to the
great and good judge:

"'The young men saw me and hid themselves, and the aged
arose and stood up.

"'The princes refrained from talking, and laid their hand
upon their mouth.

"'When the ear heard me, then it blessed me, and when the
eye saw me, it gave witness to me.

"'Because I delivered the poor that cried, and the fatherless,
and him that had none to help him.

"'The blessing of him that was ready to perish came upon
me, and I caused the widow's heart to sing for joy.

"'I put on righteousness, and it clothed me. My judgment
was as a robe and a diadem. I was eyes to the blind, and feet
was I to the lame.

"'I was a father to the poor, and the cause which I knew not
I searched out.

"'And I brake the jaws of the wicked, and I plucked the
spoil out of his teeth.'

"Give to the community such a judge, and
I care little who makes the rest of the Constitution,
or what party administers it. It will be a free government I know. Let us repose secure under the
shade of a learned, impartial, and trusted magis-
tracy, and we need no more."

There may be paragraphs in oratory, both ancient and modern, either more concise in expression, or more elevated in character, or more sublime
in the precepts taught, or more brilliant in imagery,
but in ease and ingenuity of argument, in aptness

of illustration, in fertility of language and beauty of diction combined, these passages may well challenge comparison with the best selections from argumentative orations.

Nor let it be forgotten that, for more than a third of a century, in a professional practice which was vast from the beginning to the end, Mr. Choate exhibited constantly like qualities and powers.

A lay-member of the convention assigned as a reason for favoring an elective judiciary that, in some cases, as he alleged, erroneous decisions had been pronounced from the bench. Mr. Choate thus dealt with the objection, and thus closed his speech :

" I have lost a good many cases, first and last, and I hope to try and expect to lose a good many more ; but I never heard a client in my life, however dissatisfied with the verdict or the charge, say a word about changing the tenure of the judicial office. I greatly doubt if I have heard as many as three express themselves dissatisfied with the judge ; though, times without number, they have regretted that he found himself compelled to go against them. My own tenure I have often thought in danger ; but I am yet to see the first client who thought of meddling with that of the court. What is true of those clients is true of the whole people of Massachusetts. Sir, that people have two traits of character—just as our political system, in which

that character is shown forth, has two great ends.
They love liberty ; that is one trait. They love it,
and they possess it to their hearts' content. Free
as storms to-day do they know it and feel it, every
one of them, from the sea to the Green Mountains.
But there is another side to their character, and
that is the old Anglo-Saxon instinct of property ;
the rational and the creditable desire to be secure
in life, in reputation, in the earnings of daily labor,
in the little all which makes up the treasures and the
dear charities of the humblest home, the desire to
feel certain that when they come to die the last will
shall be kept, the smallest legacy of affection shall
reach its object, although the giver is in his grave ;
this desire, and the sound sense to know that a
learned, impartial, and honored judiciary is the only
means of having it indulged. They have nothing
timorous in them, as touching the largest liberty.
They rather like the exhilaration of crowding sail on
the noble old ship, and giving her to scud away before a fourteen-knot breeze ; but they know, too,
that if the storm comes on to blow, and the masts
go overboard, and the gun-deck is rolled under
water, and the lee-shore, edged with foam, thunders
under her stern, that the sheet-anchor and best
bower then are everything ! Give them good
ground-tackle, and they will carry her round the
world and back again, till there shall be no more
sea."

In this extract there is an exuberance of illustration which passes the limits set by critics and

careful writers, yet it was not only tolerated, it was applauded by the ablest body of men ever assembled in Massachusetts.

But, whatever may be the estimate of Mr. Choate's career in the field of politics and statesmanship, it was his ambition to rule the twelve men upon the panel, and his triumphs were won at the bar. His vocation was the law; politics and statesmanship were avocations to which he turned temporarily for relaxation, or under a sense of duty to the public. To these, however, he never gave his mind continuously and without reserve, nor lent his powers in all their fullness.

Of the objects of human ambition, the purpose to rule the twelve men upon the panel may not be the highest, but it is an honorable object, and in the case of Mr. Choate it was the object to which his talents and genius were best adapted.

The highest secular pursuit is statesmanship—the government of a country. Those who frame constitutions and make laws are of the higher department; those who interpret and administer the laws, both constitutional and statute laws, are in the second department, but each department is equally important to the public welfare. The ability to frame constitutions and to enact laws implies the capacity to discern legal distinctions, and the learning and skill to protect rights and to remedy wrongs by systematic agencies.

It is the object of governments to regulate the relations of men to men, and of men to things, upon ethical principles capable of general application. The study of those principles and of their application in different countries and in different ages is the work of the lawyer and the necessity of the statesman. Hence it is that in every country the rule of the lawyer begins where and when the rule of the soldier ends — not the rule of the professional lawyer exclusively, but of such as have legal perceptions and that training which enables them to apply legal principles in public affairs. In all governments the end sought is dictated by the ruling force, whether the body of the people, as in some countries, or the hereditary dynasty, as in others.

In English-speaking countries, the statesman devises the laws, the judge interprets them, and the jury applies them in all courts of law, and not infrequently in courts of equity. Thus, finally, the protection of the rights of liberty, property, and reputation is confided to the twelve men upon the panel. Hence the wisdom of the observation made by Brougham that "all we see about us, kings, lords, and commons, the whole machinery of the state, all the apparatus of the system and its various workings, end in simply bringing twelve good men into a box." * But how are the twelve good men to find the truth ? The judge knows nothing of the case ; the jury know nothing of the case. The attorneys and advocates are the eyes and ears of the court—the agencies that develop the facts in the presence of judge and jury, and thus enable the judge to apply the law, and the jury to find the facts.

If deprived of the agency and aid of attorneys, the courts of justice would soon lose their value. By jury-trials, the rights of men are decided, and, as a verdict is not a precedent, the evils result-ing from error are limited to the case at bar. The rule of the twelve is a limited rule ; but the decis-ions of the twelve, when massed and considered together, touch and control nearly all the contro-verted questions of society.

In this view of the importance of jury-trials, it was not a low ambition, nor an unworthy purpose, which led Mr. Choate to select that forum for the development and exhibition of his powers, talents, and genius.

The questions submitted to a jury are often questions of magnitude, in a public sense, and they are always questions of present and pressing im-

---

* " Present State of the Law," February 7, 1823.

portance to the parties concerned. In the inves-
tigations incident to and necessary in the trial of
causes, not only is a knowledge of the law required,
but a knowledge also of the arts, industries, and
sciences of the world is essential to the advocate.
Beyond these qualifications even, there is a field for
the use—I do not say display—but a field for the
use of every variety of learning that can be gathered by the most diligent student. In all these ac-
quisitions, Mr. Choate was the best-equipped advocate ever known by the American bar.

For half a century he pursued his studies, special and general, in season and out of season, by
day and by night, denying himself pleasures, amusements, relaxations even, dividing his time between
his library and the court-room.

The Bible was a book of constant study, and
his devotion to the New Testament in Greek led
Mr. Webster to say, as he examined the books upon
the shelves of Mr. Choate's library, " Thirteen edi-
tions of the Greek Testament, and not one copy of
the Constitution of your country ! " He translated
the Greek and Latin classics, studied French law
and history in the language, and in English he read
everything from the Black-Letter to Dickens. The
four great men of England, in his estimation and in
their order, were Shakespeare, Bacon, Milton, and
Burke. Indulging in exaggeration, he wrote to

3

Sumner, " Out of Burke might be cut fifty Mack-
intoshes, one hundred and seventy-five Macaulays,
forty Jeffreys, and two hundred and fifty Sir Robert
Peels, and leave him greater than Pitt and Fox together."

With a mind so given to exaggeration, it is
difficult to realize that he was a close — not a
concise, but a close—logical reasoner, whose arguments, whether to court or jury, were seldom
overloaded or embarrassed by imagery or illustrations.

Logic is the one quality, the one power, absolutely essential to the advocate. Without this there
can be no success. There are advocates, however,
usually men of an inferior sort, but sometimes they
are men at once able and disingenuous, whose arguments are logical in the parts but illogical in
their combinations. Mr. Choate's arguments were
logical in the parts and logical in the whole. His
competitors in the field of logic were Mason, Webster, and Curtis, and he was the equal of either of
them in the propriety and scientific arrangement
of his arguments, though not in the power of statement; but in learning, in genius, in the capacity to
weave and unweave the webs of human testimony,
he was superior to either of these men, as he was to
all the lawyers of America of the generations to
which they belonged.

In addressing a court upon questions of law, or even upon mixed questions of law and fact, it is both wise and safe to limit the discussion to pivotal propositions—those propositions on which the case must be decided. In this faculty, Judge Curtis excelled ; but so predominant was this quality in him as to impair essentially his standing as a jury-lawyer. In Mr. Webster, the logical power, the power of statement, wealth of imagination, and purity and splendor of diction, were so combined as to render him equally formidable before the court and to the jury. But Mr. Choate excelled Mr. Webster in the variety and extent of his learning, in the facility and genius that he displayed in the cross-examination of witnesses — a field in which causes are sometimes won, but more frequently lost—in his resources of argument, often designed to meet the peculiarities of individual jurors, and in his ability to repeat a thought with new illustrations, and in a diction at once fresh and attractive.

Much may be assumed of a court, but of a jury it can not be assumed that secondary considerations may not have great weight, and therefore the skillful advocate will sometimes dwell upon insignificant topics, and in different forms present his views to the various men upon the panel. In all these things Mr. Choate was unsurpassed, and yet so great were his powers that his arguments were never tedious, even to those who thought further discussion unnecessary.

It is the misfortune of many men of large reading, that, in the use of the knowledge thus acquired, they show their dependence upon notes and commonplace-books—those aids to inferior intellects and hindrances to growth in the young. What Mr. Choate read he assimilated to himself, so that in its use there were no betrayals of the sources. His quotations were not many, and generally they were brief and so apt that their omission seemed impossible. When commonplace-books are discarded by the student, he will then become self-reliant, and read with the purpose of holding in his memory whatever may be worth possessing.

Mr. Choate seemed never to forget anything, and his practice of writing his arguments served to fix in his memory what he wrote, or to aid him in reproducing it. But this habit must have been due to a purpose, inasmuch as his power as an *extempore* speaker was not only adequate to all the exigencies of professional life, but no distinction could be made between his written and his unwritten arguments.

At the end the test of greatness is success. A single triumph is not success either in the field or the forum; but a series of victories due always to

plan, courage, and brilliancy of execution place
the actor above the region of criticism as to
the presence of extraordinary powers. Traits of
weakness there may be, errors there may be,
deficiencies there may be, but the whole must be
accepted as a form of greatness that neither enemies nor critics can disturb.

For more than a quarter of a century Mr.
Choate was accustomed to deal with the most
important causes pending in the tribunals of the
country, and of every form known to our system
of jurisprudence, and always he was equal to the
cause and to the opposing advocate. Of the great
lawyers of this country, after Mr. Webster, whose
greatness as a lawyer was an inherent quality of
his greatness as a man, Mr. Pinckney and Mr.
Wirt would be first named. In a comparison of
the three, it is to be said that Mr. Choate had all
the logical power required by the case, and that in
learning, in resources and ingenuity of argument,
in exuberance of diction, in aptness and splendor of
illustration, neither Pinckney nor Wirt can be compared with Choate.

There is a quality of poetry, and it is neither
the measure nor the rhythm, that not only adorns
prose arguments, but enlightens the understand-
ings of those who listen and those who read. The
speech of Antony over the body of Cæsar may be

so condensed as at the same time to preserve the logic and destroy the effect.

In comparing the printed speeches of Wirt and Pinckney with the printed speeches of Choate, some allowance ought to be made in favor of the first two, although it is probable that Wirt himself reported his argument in the case of Gibbons and ' Ogden, and Pinckney may have done the same in the case of Hodges. Mr. Choate was a rapid speaker, and the reporters were not always able to follow him. Of the report of his argument in the Dalton case he said, " Not verbally, not verbally, but the general nonsense of the thing they have got."

Of English advocates neither Erskine nor Curran nor North, who most resembled Choate in style, can be compared with him in learning, whether in the law or in general literature ; and the testimony of the printed speeches is that he excelled them all in grace of diction, in ingenuity of argument, and in the capacity to command the aid of the better sentiments of the mind and the more elevating passions of the human heart without awakening suspicion or arousing opposition by a statement of the end sought, or by a suggestion of the purpose in view. If Brougham's superior learning be admitted, and in the law and general literature it is not easy to imagine such superiority, the fact remains that, in ease of composition, in the resources of argument, in imagination, and in diction, he was far inferior to Choate.

In a letter to Zachary Macaulay, in which he gave advice for the education of the son, afterward Lord Macaulay, Brougham says that he wrote the peroration of his defense of Queen Caroline nineteen times before its delivery. Of Choate nothing of the sort was true. He was in the habit of transfixing passing thoughts and fugitive sentences by writing, and for this purpose he often left his bed in the night. Such passages may have been rewritten in his speeches and arguments, but there is no reason to suppose that beyond this he subjected himself to the labor of revising and re-writing.

Many years since I attended a meeting of the Boston Scientific Club, at the house of Mr. Thomas G. Carey. Mr. Carey was a gentleman of wealth and taste, and his rooms were adorned with paintings and works of art in which he was a connoisseur. The evening was given to an essay upon paintings, by Mr. Carey. Of that essay I have preserved one thought only—that the finest paintings are produced by the smallest outlay of pigment and the fewest strokes of the brush. And it is true that the absolutely great things in art, in war, and in literature, are the products of absolutely great men and by the ordinary movements of great minds.

It is impossible to associate the thought of study, or of what we call intellectual effort, with the Sermon on the Mount.

The writings of Shakespeare show no marks of paring and cutting, of reconstruction and rewriting. It is otherwise, however, with Bacon, Milton, Addison, Johnson, Byron, and Brougham.

Of Choate's many arguments, only a few are preserved, but they were prepared at the moment and under the pressure of business. In great causes he had many days, and not infrequently weeks, for thought, but his time was occupied necessarily in the trial itself, leaving only spare moments and the night for the work of preparation.

Mr. Choate's powers and resources are best displayed in the report of the Dalton trial. This was a libel for divorce by Frank Dalton against his wife, Helen Maria Dalton, born Gove.

Mrs. Dalton was the daughter of a retired merchant, and was married to Dalton in the year 1855, and at the age of about eighteen years. Soon after her marriage she became intimate with a young man named Sumner, which led finally to a confession on her part, but of such a nature as to be open to two interpretations. It led, however, to an attack upon Sumner by Dalton, which was fol-

lowed by the death of Sumner, the arrest and im-
prisonment of Dalton for manslaughter, and his
conviction finally of a simple assault. Until about
the time of Dalton's release from prison, he accepted his wife's statement as an admission of
frivolity and indiscretion, of which she had re-
pented bitterly; but his associations or reflections,
or both together, wrought an entire change in his
feelings and opinions, and he came finally to regard
his wife's confession as an admission of guilt. At
the trial, two persons, who were present at the
confession, so represented the interview between
Dalton and his wife. The cross-examination of
these witnesses by Mr. Durant, and the argument
of Mr. Choate, destroyed their testimony utterly.

Never in any cause were the genius and nobil-
ity of an advocate more conspicuous than in Mr.
Choate in that contest. He did not aim merely to
satisfy the twelve men upon the panel that Mrs.
Dalton was innocent, but it was his higher purpose to satisfy Dalton that she was worthy to
be his wife, and it has been said that this purpose he accomplished — and all against heavy
odds.

There were two swift witnesses, one of them
the brother-in-law of Dalton, to report the confession; and a wet-nurse, to testify to an attempt
on the part of Mrs. Dalton to destroy the fruit of

her crime. The witnesses, one after another, were extinguished literally, and Dalton was brought finally to accept the advocate's view of the case.

Twice in the exordium of his argument does he declaim against the folly of Mrs. Dalton, coupled with a denial of the crime charged in the libel. This is the refrain of his discourse, but always in fresh language, as though the thought itself had never before been used. Thus he commences:

"Mr. Foreman and Gentlemen: I congratulate you on approaching, at least, the close of this case, so severe and painful to all of us. One effort more of your indulgence I have to ask, and then we shall retire from your presence, satisfied and grateful that everything which candor and patience and intelligence can do for these afflicted suitors has been done.

"It very rarely indeed happens, gentlemen, in the trial of a civil controversy, that both parties have an equal, or rather a vast interest that one of them—in this case the defendant—should be clearly proved to be entitled to your verdict. Unusual as it is, in the view I take of this case, such a one is now on trial.

"To both of these parties it is of supreme importance, in the view that I take of it, that you should find this young wife, erring, indiscreet, imprudent, forgetful of herself, if it be so, but innocent of the last and the greatest crime of a married woman. I say to both parties it is important. I cannot deny, of course, gentlemen, that her interest in such a result is perhaps the greater of the two. For her, indeed, it is not at all too much to say that everything is staked upon the result. I can not, of course, hope, I can not say, that any verdict which you can render in this case can give her back again the happy and sunny life which seemed opening upon her two years ago ; I can not say it, because I do not think that any verdict you can render will ever enable her to recall those weeks of folly, and frivolity, and vanity without a blush, without a tear ; I can not desire that it should be so. But, gentlemen, whether these grave and impressive proceedings shall terminate by sending this young wife from your presence with the scarlet letter upon her brow ; whether in this, her morning of life, her name shall be thus publicly stricken from the roll of virtuous women, her whole future darkened by dishonor and waylaid by temptation ; her companions driven from her side ; herself cast out, it may be, upon common society, the sport of libertines, unassisted by public opinion, or sympathy, or self-respect—this certainly rests with you. For her, therefore, I am surely warranted in saying that more than her life is here at stake. Whatsoever things are honest, whatsoever things are lovely, whatsoever things are pure, whatsoever things are of good report, if there be any virtue, if there be any praise, all the chances that are to be left her in life, for winning and holding these holy, beautiful, and needful things, rest with you. . . . But is there not another person, gentlemen, interested in these proceedings, with an equal or

at least a supreme interest with the respondent, that
you shall be able by your verdict to say that Helen
Dalton is not guilty of the crime of adultery, and is
not that person her husband? I do not say, gentlemen, that he ought to feel or would feel grateful
for a verdict that should acquit her on any ground
of doubt or technicality, leaving everybody to sus-
pect her guilty ; I do not say that he would feel
contented with such a verdict as that, though I say
it would be her sacred right that such a verdict
should be rendered, if your minds were left in that
state. He must acquiesce whether the verdict is
satisfactory to him in that particular or not. But,
gentlemen, if you can here and now, on this evidence, acquit your consciences and render a verdict
that shall assure this husband that a jury of.Suffolk,
men of honor and spirit, some of them his personal
friends, believe that he has been the victim of a
cruel and groundless jealousy; that they believe
that he has been led by that scandal that circulates
about him, and has influenced him everywhere;
that he has been made to misconceive the nature
and overestimate the extent of the injury his wife
has done him ; if he could be made to believe and
see, as I believe you see and believe, and every
other human being sees and believes, that the story
by which he has been induced to institute these
proceedings is falser than the coinage of hell; if
you can thus enable him to see that, without dishonor, he may again take her to his bosom, let me
ask you if any other human being can do another
so great a kindness as this?"

And thus Mr. Choate went on through two full days, analyzing the evidence, crushing the adverse witnesses, explaining disagreeable facts, admitting and condemning the conduct of his client, but always denying the extreme guilt charged, and all with a splendor of diction and ingenuity of argument to which the present generation of the *habitués* of court-houses are strangers.

Never, elsewhere, not even in works of ethics or romance, were the nature and evils of flirtation so set forth and at once condemned, explained, and, in a degree, excused. Near the close of the argument, Mr. Choate said :

" I leave her case, therefore, upon this statement, and respectfully submit that, for both their sakes, you will render a verdict promptly and joyfully in favor of Helen Dalton—for both their sakes. There is a future for them both together, I think ; but if that be not so—if it be that this matter has proceeded so far that her husband's affections have been alienated, and that a happy life in her case has become impracticable, yet, for all that, let there be no divorce. For no levity, no vanity, no indiscretion, let there be a divorce. . . . If they may not be dismissed then, gentlemen, to live again together, for her sake and her parents', sustain her ; give her back to self-respect and the assistance of that public opinion which all of us require."

He closed with a quotation from one of Mrs.

Dalton's letters to her husband: "Wishing you much happiness and peace, with much love, if you will accept it, I remain your wife," and added:

"So may she remain until that one of them to whom it is appointed first to die, shall find the peace of the grave!"

As the Dalton case was the outcome of human passions, so in the trial there were constant appeals to the sympathies of the jury and the public.

In the defense, Mr. Choate was not merely the advocate; his nature was such that he defended Mrs. Dalton as though she had been his daughter or sister.

But let it not be imagined that his success lay in the nature and circumstances of the cause. He was equally great upon constitutional questions, in the domain of the common law, the patent law, and in admiralty.

He died in the fullness of his powers, when he was less than sixty years of age, free from any stain on his personal character, and with no just imputation on his professional career. Endowed as he was by nature with wonderful powers for labor, for the acquisition of knowledge, and gifted as he was in all the arts of oratory, he takes rank with the ablest advocates who have honored and illustrated the profession of the law in modern times. Most men in the profession toil for a living, or for money, or for the transitory fame which sometimes attends the career of a successful lawyer.

Mr. Choate studied law as a science and practiced it as an art. He was indifferent to money, indifferent to fame. He neglected the care of his arguments and speeches, and he made only imperfect and desultory records of his services. Until his association with his son-in-law, Mr. Bell, his income was only sufficient to meet his moderate expenditures in everything except books. In 1851 I called at his house in the evening for professional consultation, and with me went a country lawyer who was not accustomed to the large libraries of modern times. We were taken into Mr. Choate's library, which filled two rooms in the second story of the house. The partition had been cut away, and thus at one glance we could see the extent of the library, the files of books rising to the ceiling, and occupying the larger part of the floor. Said my associate, in amazement, " What a collection of books you have, Mr. Choate ! "

" Yes—more than I have paid for ; but that is the bookseller's business, not mine." This was an exhibition of his habit of extravagance in statement. Let us not infer that he was indifferent to

his pecuniary obligations, although he was indifferent to money as a possession.

In an acquaintance of nearly twenty years, I
was led to esteem Mr. Choate, perhaps to admire
him. Long ago I gave a half promise to myself
that I would make a mark upon the sands of time,
though slight it might be, as a tribute to his genius.
From that acquaintance I received the impression
that he was the ablest jury-lawyer that America
had then seen. Since his death I have had other
twenty years for observation and reflection, and
I announce my conclusion in one half-sentence—
that, for all the varied exigencies of professional
life, Rufus Choate was the best-equipped advocate
who ever stood in a judicial forum and spoke the
English language.

All this, and yet Mr. Choate's greatness was not
of the absolute. It was a greatness achieved. It
bore no relation to the supremacy of Shakespeare
who spurned teachers and schools, and who for
nearly three centuries has controlled art in literature and defied criticism. Mr. Choate's greatness
had only a remote relation to that of Webster, of
whom it may be said that we can not imagine a
condition of society in which his superiority would
not have been recognized, even if the training of
the schools had been wanting.

Mr. Choate, however, is a conspicuous example

of the influence of schools and culture upon a man
of genius endowed with the virtue of industry ;
and his career is an earnest, a sufficient protest
against the opinion that the schools and universities should not teach all literature as well as all
science, and in that literature all languages in which
its gems are found or which contribute to the language that we speak. Not everything in literature
and science for everybody ; but there should be
somebody for everything, and, that there may be
somebody for everything, everything should be
taught.

4

DANIEL WEBSTER.

In the month of January, 1839, I made my first visit to the city of Washington, and for the first time I then saw and heard Mr. Webster. He had reached the summit of his fame as an orator, and it was then that in personal appearance he fully justified the encomium bestowed upon him by his friends and admirers who had crowned him "the godlike Daniel."

I heard him make one or two brief commonplace observations in the Senate, but I had also the privilege of hearing his argument before the Supreme Court in the case of Smith *vs.* Richards, reported in volume thirteen of Peters's reports. His opponent was Mr. Crittenden, of Kentucky.

Mr. Webster appeared for the appellant, who had appealed from the decree of the Circuit Court for the Southern District of New York, by which a contract for the sale of a gold-mine in Virginia had been annulled, upon the ground that the vender (Smith) made false representations at the time of the sale in regard to material facts.

The decree of the Circuit Court was affirmed by the Supreme Court, three of the nine judges —Story, McLean, and Baldwin—dissenting. Of these nine judges, only three—Taney, Story, and McLean—are now known, even to the profession. Yet to an inexperienced person it was an awe-inspiring tribunal. Nor has the impression then produced upon me been removed by time and experience. In like manner the court will establish and maintain its power over many successive generations of American citizens. If the court shall ever be in peril, its peril will be due to politics—to the disposition of its members either to mingle in the political contests of the time, or to seek political distinction and office. Happily, thus far in our history, the small number of judges who have attempted to step from the bench to the presidency have been disappointed.

Speaking only of the past, it is to be noted as a singular circumstance that the three most distinguished judges were active politicians when they were appointed.

Marshall, Story, and Taney were pronounced partisans, and upon political questions their opinions as judges, were shaped or modified usually by the views of the politician. The contrary could not have been anticipated. It would not often happen that a Federalist and a State-rights

Democrat would agree upon questions testing the scope of the powers of the national Government.

It is the boast of a class of lawyers—not a numerous class—that they seldom or never lose a cause. Such has not been the experience of the greatest nor of the purest of the profession. And assuredly such was not Mr. Webster's experience. Without claiming that I have made a complete examination of the reports, it is safe to assume that Mr. Webster failed in one half of the causes that he argued in the Supreme Court of the United States in the period of his largest practice.

With the increase of business, and with the increase of the instruments and agencies for the transaction of business, new questions will arise inevitably. On those questions differences of opinion must exist.

The general public is inclined to accept the notion that an attorney is inexcusable, if he advises a suit in a bad cause, and that an advocate is worthy of stripes if he defends a wicked client, or appears on the wrong side of a contested case. In presence of the circumstance that there are differences of opinion in courts, sometimes upon questions of pure law, sometimes upon the admissibility of testimony, and sometimes upon the value of evidence, it is not strange that attorneys and

THE STATESMAN. 47

advocates, in advance of the trial and the tests of judicial proceedings, are unable to estimate with certainty the character of the causes that they are called to promote or to defend.

Again, I heard Mr. Webster at the completion of the Bunker Hill Monument, June 17, 1843. He was then in his sixty-second year, but time had not made any impression upon his vigorous physical organization, and his oratorical powers were unimpaired. He spoke to an audience that stretched far beyond the power of any merely human voice. It was, however, an audience in full sympathy with the occasion and with the speaker. It was the last considerable gathering of the survivors of the War of the Revolution. They numbered but one hundred and eight. At the dedication of the Acton Monument, in 1851, only two of that number survived; and at the reception of the Prince of Wales, in 1859, there remained of those who fought at Bunker Hill only a Mr. Farnham, whose life had been extended to about one hundred years.

Mr. Webster had been called by President Harrison to the head of the Cabinet in 1841, and he continued in the office of the Secretary of the Department of State under President Tyler until May, 1843.

By his adherence to President Tyler he alienated his followers in Massachusetts, and in September, 1842, the Whig State Convention declared "a full and final separation" between the Whig party and the President.   Mr. Webster treated this action as a censure of himself.   In that he did not err; but he was not then disposed to submit to the censure without answer, nor even without resistance and threats of retaliation.   His friends called a meeting in Faneuil Hall.   The meeting was held September 30.   The mayor of the city presided. In the preceding August the Ashburton Treaty had been signed.   The apprehensions of war growing out of the northeastern boundary controversy were quieted, and Mr. Webster had thus arrested the adverse drift of public sentiment.   The mayor, in his introductory address, said that Mr. Webster might "be left to take care of his own honor and reputation."   With emphasis Mr. Webster adopted the remark, and then proceeded to say that, as he must bear the consequences of the decision, he had "better be trusted to make it."   He asserted his right to be counted as a Whig, and he intimated that, if the issue were pressed, he would appeal to the State of Massachusetts.   His opponents were not ready for an appeal to the State, and the tendency of public sentiment was again in Mr. Webster's favor.   He resigned his seat in the Cabinet in May, 1843, and in 1845 he was again elected a

member of the Senate, and by the representatives
of the Whig party that had denounced him in
1842.

At the time of his election, Mr. Webster had
re-established his supremacy over the Whig party,
although the division between "conscience Whigs"
and "cotton Whigs" was visible.

The differences between the two wings of the
party culminated in 1848 in the secession of the
anti-slavery men, who supported Van Buren and
Adams in the election of that year.

At the opening of the January session of the
Legislature of Massachusetts for the year 1847,
Fletcher Webster, the eldest of Mr. Webster's
sons, took his seat in the House of Representatives
as a member from the city of Boston.

Caleb Cushing was returned from the town of
Newburyport. Mr. Cushing had been a Whig.
He was a member of Congress at the time of
President Tyler's defection, when he became one
of the Tyler body-guard, or Omnibus party, as the
supporters of Tyler in the national House of Representatives were called. In November, 1846,
when he was elected to the Legislature, he had
only recently returned from China, where, as
commissioner appointed by President Tyler, he
had negotiated an important treaty with that
country.

On the first day of the session of the Legislature, Mr. Cushing introduced a resolution to appropriate twenty thousand dollars to aid in equipping
a regiment for the war in Mexico. The regiment
had been raised, the company-officers had been
chosen, and Mr. Cushing had either been appointed
colonel, or there was a general impression that he
was to have the command. Money, however, was
more necessary than officers. The war was un-
popular in Massachusetts, and the Whig party,
with here and there an exception, was hostile to
the appropriation.

The resolution was sent to a special committee,
of which Mr. Cushing was the chairman, and of
which I was made a member. According to the
then prevailing custom, the committee was composed, in the majority, of friends of the measure.
Consequently, the resolution was reported, with a
recommendation in its favor.

Mr. Webster's youngest son, Edward, was a
captain in the regiment. It was natural, therefore,
that Fletcher Webster should support the resolution. It was understood, also, that Mr. Webster
favored the appropriation. In the discussion,
Fletcher Webster made one remark that indicated the presence of his father's blood. In urg-
ing the passage of the resolution, he assured his
Whig associates that they would be required to

explain their votes against the appropriation, and he then said, with emphasis, " and explanations are always disagreeable."

Fletcher Webster was a man of more than ordinary ability, but he was weighted by his father's pre-eminence, and he realized, whenever he spoke, that comparisons were instituted to his disadvantage. Again, while he was not under the average of men in height and weight, he felt his inferiority to his father in these particulars ; and he once said to me that a man could "come to but little unless he was of good size and appearance."

The acquaintance I thus formed with Fletcher Webster may have been the cause of some kindnesses which Mr. Webster extended to me.

Within a few weeks after Mr. Webster delivered his speech of the 7th of March, 1850, he visited Boston, and took rooms at the Revere House. The Legislature was then in session, and J. Thomas Stevenson, as the friend of Mr. Webster, gave informal invitations to members to call upon Mr. Webster on an evening named.

His speech of the 7th of March had alienated the Whigs generally, and a small number only ventured to call upon their old chief. The Democratic members of the Legislature were free from constraint. I called with others, and it was then that I was introduced to him. He wore the dress

known as his court dress. Time had wrought
great changes in the seven preceding years. His
form was erect, his hair retained its dark color,
but he had lost flesh, his cheeks were sunken, and
the black circles around his large eyes were more
distinct than they had been in 1843. The marks
of physical beauty had disappeared, but the evidences of majesty of person and greatness of intellect remained. As I stood before him I estimated
his height, which was then less than five feet and
eleven inches. His speech of the 7th of March
had destroyed his hold upon the Whig party of the
State, and it had destroyed the hold of the Whig
party upon the State itself.

During this visit Mr. Webster's friends peti-
tioned the city government for the use of Faneuil
Hall, that Mr. Webster might explain and defend
his speech of the 7th of March.

The prayer of the petition was rejected. The
city government was in the hands of the Whig
party, and John P. Bigelow, whose sister was the
wife of Abbott Lawrence, was the mayor. The
responsibility for the indignity was laid upon Mr.
Lawrence and the wing of the party that he represented. To Mr. Webster Faneuil Hall was consecrated ground, and the refusal of the city government to open its doors to him and his friends was
an indignity which he never forgot and which he

never forgave. The act of the city government was not only unwise — it was an act for which there was neither defense nor excuse. For a third of a century Mr. Webster had been the chief personage in Massachusetts, and in intellectual power he was the first person in the republic.

He had defended Massachusetts in her history; he had again and again vindicated her public policy; and the city of Boston was largely indebted to him for its business prosperity and for its eminent rank and influence in the councils of the nation. If his speech had been much more offensive than it was, the city which he had represented and honored, and to which he was deeply attached, should have given him an opportunity to explain and defend the course that he had chosen to pursue.

In the month of September, 1851, railway communication with Canada was established, and the State of Massachusetts and the city of Boston joined in celebrating the event.

Mr. Webster was then Secretary of State under President Fillmore. The President and three members of his Cabinet, Webster, Stuart, and Conrad, accepted the invitation to be present. Lord Elgin, Governor-General of Canada; Sir Francis Hincks, Attorney - General; Mr. Joseph Howe, of Nova Scotia, and other colonial officials, were present. Mr. Webster arrived in Boston several days in ad-

vance of the President, and took rooms at the
Revere House. When I called upon him he said
that he should cheerfully appear, if invited to do
so, whenever the State appeared, but that he should
have nothing to do with the city. He also said
that upon the arrival of the President it would be
a pleasure to him to introduce the members of the
State government.

Upon the arrival of Mr. Fillmore, the members
of the State government went to the Revere House
at about one o'clock in the afternoon. We were
met by Mr. Stevenson, who informed Mr. Webster
of our presence. He soon appeared, dressed in his
court suit. We passed to the reception room,
where we found Mayor Bigelow engaged in intro-
ducing the members of the city government. Mr.
Webster paid no attention to the mayor, but he
took possession of the floor, and in a loud voice he
proceeded to announce the names of the gentlemen
that he had in charge.

His only apparent regret was the fact that they
were not more numerous. It is difficult to comprehend the *hauteur* of Mr. Webster's bearing, or the
weight of the indignity that he heaped upon the
mayor and his associates. Mr. Webster was entitled to precedence, but he asserted himself as
though the mayor were an offensive intruder and
too low or too base for notice.

The day following our introduction the President and the members of his Cabinet were received by the State authorities. It fell to me to make a speech of welcome. I prepared my speech, and gave it to the newspapers, but by an oversight, which I can not explain, I omitted all reference to Mr. Webster, although I had given a sentence to his associates who were present. At about eleven o'clock in the morning the fact of the omission occurred to me. I then prepared a paragraph, and sent it to the printers.

At the reception the President was upon my right upon the dais, Secretaries Conrad and Stuart sat upon his right, and Mr. Webster had a seat upon my left. Neither Conrad nor Stuart gave any recognition of my allusion to them; but when I referred to Mr. Webster, he rose from his seat immediately, and in return the immense audience responded with cheers such as had often greeted him in his brightest days. In that act he exhibited the quality of the gentleman and the skill of the actor.

In his speech in reply he gave a very distinct indorsement to my administration of the affairs of the State, but not upon partisan grounds. The election in 1851 was hotly contested, and I attribute my success to the support which Mr. Webster gave to me in that speech and privately to his friends.

In the month of May, 1852, the clergy of the Methodist Church held a National Convention in Boston. Mr. Webster was invited to make an address to the convention. The meeting was held in Faneuil Hall. It was Mr. Webster's last appearance on that historical stage. He was then a candidate for the presidency. It was understood that the occasion was designed to promote his ambition in that respect, but the time had passed when his appearance in public could advance his political fortunes. Age, disappointments, and disease had wrought terrible changes in his condition and appearance. His form was wasted, his voice, once electric and commanding, had lost its power and cadence, and his intellectual faculties were slow in movement and lacking in force. In the reception-room he welcomed his old friend Thomas H. Perkins, in the tones of voice which in former days had charmed audiences that took but little interest in his methodical arguments. Mr. Webster had prepared the heads of his remarks upon sheets of note-paper, and his son Fletcher sat in front of him, and handed the sheets to his father, one by one, as the topics were treated. There were a few occasions when Mr. Webster's voice rang through the hall with something of its old-time force and tones, but generally he could not be heard at the distance of twenty feet. Indeed, many of his words were inaudible to those who were upon the platform.

The ambition of Mr. Webster and of his friends was not promoted by his appearance upon a stage where in his better days he had achieved many signal triumphs.

Mr. Webster returned to Washington, where he awaited the action of the Whig Convention that assembled at Baltimore. There can be no doubt that the nomination of General Scott was a severe disappointment. That he should have anticipated his own nomination is an additional evidence of the infatuation which takes possession of men whose thoughts are directed to the presidency. Mr. Webster's friends, and probably Mr. Webster himself, anticipated that the South would recognize its obligation for his speech of the 7th of March, 1850. From the South, however, he received no support. His disappointment must have been bitter, but his " midnight speech," as it was called, was a masterpiece of self-control under trying circumstances, and an exhibition of his genius as an orator, which equaled the best efforts of his best days.

Upon the nomination of General Scott his friends called upon him for a speech, and after listening to him they called upon Mr. Webster, in the hope that they might obtain his indorsement of the proceedings.

He was then impaired seriously in health and in spirits he was broken completely. His speech is worthy of notice as a singularly graceful effort, and as the last brilliant spark of his expiring genius:

"I thank you, fellow-citizens, for your friendly and respectful call. I am very glad to see you.

"Some of you have been engaged in an arduous public duty at Baltimore, the object of your meeting being the selection of a fit person to be supported for the office of President of the United States. Others of you take an interest in the result of the deliberations of that assembly of Whigs. It so happened that my name among others was presented on the occasion. Another candidate, however, was preferred.

"I have only to say, gentlemen, that the convention did, I doubt not, what it thought best, and exercised its discretion in the important matter committed to it. The result has caused me no personal feeling whatever, nor any change of conduct or purpose.

" What I have been I am in principle and in character; and what I am, I hope to continue to be.

" Circumstances or opponents may triumph over my fortunes, but they will not triumph over my temper or my self-respect.

" Gentlemen, this is a serene and beautiful night. Ten thousand thousand of the lights of heaven illuminate the firmament. They rule the night. A few hours hence their glory will be extinguished.

' Ye stars that glitter in the skies,
And gayly dance before my eyes,
What are ye when the sun shall rise ? '

" Gentlemen, there is not one among you who will sleep better to-night than I shall. If I wake I shall learn the hour from the constellations, and I shall rise in the morning, God willing, with the lark; and though the lark is a better songster than I am, yet he will not leave the dew and the daisies and spring upward to greet the purpling east with a more blithe and jocund spirit than I possess. Gentlemen, I again repeat my thanks for this mark of your respect, and commend you to the enjoyment of a quiet and satisfactory repose. May God bless you all ! " *

General Scott was not indorsed, the Whig party was neither applauded nor condemned, and his own purposes were carefully concealed. In his reference to the night and the stars there was a touch of sarcasm, which was repeated when he commended his hearers " to the enjoyment of a quiet and satisfactory repose."

His career as a politician was ended, and in his place as Secretary of State there remained nothing of importance to be considered.

---

* This speech was corrected by Mr. Webster and published in the Boston " Transcript," with a note that it had theretofore been printed in a mutilated form.

5

He returned to Massachusetts, broken in spirit, if not altogether crushed.

During his final illness in October, 1852, he dictated a letter to me in behalf of a neighbor, and the foreman on his farm at Marshfield, for whom he wished an appointment as justice of the peace. It was his last effort to express his thoughts or wishes upon paper. After the funeral of Mr. Webster, I received the letter with a note from Mr. Abbott, his Secretary, in which he said that Mr. Webster was unable to affix his signature to the communication.

In the case of Mr. Webster, death did not destroy nor even qualify the physical marks of his intellectual greatness. When he lay in his coffin, under the elms at Marshfield, his form appeared as majestic as when he stood upon the rostrum in Faneuil Hall. His brow was massive, his eyes were large, deep sunken, and surrounded by a dark circle. His face was emaciated, but the engraved lines of toil and care remained. He seemed a giant in repose.

In Mr. Webster great power of argument and a lofty imagination were combined. In argument he spoke as one having a right to speak and to be heard, and, if he ever descended to personalities, it was only when he was under great provocation.

In many qualities, considered individually, Mr. Webster has been surpassed; but in absolute greatness of intellect, our search for his equal must be far and wide, not only among his contemporaries, but through the whole domain of history. As Secretary of State he was not a distinguished nor even a successful administrator, and the only evidence of his originating or organizing faculty is contained in the crimes act, passed in the year 1825. There are incidents in his career which warrant the conclusion that he had a dislike to the details of business, and there can be no doubt that in the later years of his life he relied upon others even in the preparation of his arguments and speeches.

At the time of the death of Judge Story, the statement was made that among his papers were seventy-five letters from Mr. Webster asking for suggestions and opinions upon legal points and topics.

But given a case, a cause, a question, a subject for argument, and Mr. Webster was without a peer, whether he was called to the attack or the defense. His premiership does not rest upon any one speech or argument. His first great argument of historical record was made in the Dartmouth College case, in the year 1818. He was then in the thirty-seventh year of his age. He had already reached a high position as a lawyer, but it is manifest that his great faculties did not mature at an early period. His college style of writing was vicious, and we may assume that his imagination and logical faculties were not blended into harmony without the influence of time and great self-discipline.

Indeed, his Latin peroration in the Dartmouth College case could not be justified, nor would any advocate now venture upon a similar experiment in the presence of the Supreme Court of the United States. A long line of historical speeches and arguments followed, some of which contain passages of enduring value as literary productions. They can be read as lessons in the schools, and recited by the youth of the land. There are constant changes in the public taste and judgment in literary matters, and books that are read with avidity by one generation are wholly neglected by a succeeding generation; but we can not imagine a time nor a condition of society when Webster's morning drum-beat passage will lose its charm. His description of a superior human intellect in his eulogy on Adams and Jefferson is so true, so graphic, and so grand, that it must always command the admiration of the reader. Without exaggeration he has painted the scene of the murder of Captain White, and given voice to the thoughts and sentiments of the assassin, in manner and form so truthful and attractive that his words must find a place in the living literature of future times.

He created a speech for John Adams, which has deceived attentive readers and students. In the peroration to his speech in reply to Hayne, he sketched a picture of the civil war as it was seen by the succeeding generation. His fears led him to apprehend a dissolution of the Union in the event of a civil, sectional war, growing out of the system of slavery, but his hopes triumphed over his fears, and he closed with the utterance which has, as we trust, become imperishable truth : " Liberty and union, now and forever, one and inseparable."

Mr. Webster's emotional nature was strong, and, in his speech in support of General Harrison as the "log-cabin candidate," he made a touching allusion to his birthplace and to the devotion of his father to his home and his country.

By way of ridicule and reproach, the Democratic party had styled General Harrison the "log-cabin candidate."

The Whig party accepted the designation, and it became the watchword of the canvass and the sign under which the party triumphed. Said Mr. Webster :

"Let him be the log-cabin candidate. What you say in scorn, we will shout with all our lungs!"

He then turned to reflections suggested by his own experience:

"It did not happen to me to be born in a log-cabin; but my elder brothers and sisters were born in a log-cabin, raised amid the snow-drifts of New Hampshire, at a period so early that, when the smoke first rose from its rude chimney, and curled over the frozen hills, there was no similar evidence of a white man's habitation between it and the settlements on the rivers of Canada. . . . I weep to think that none of those who inhabited it are now among the living; and if ever I am ashamed of it, or if I ever fail in affectionate veneration for him who reared it, and defended it against savage violence and destruction, cherished all the domestic virtues beneath its roof, and, through the fire and blood of a seven years' Revolutionary War, shrunk from no danger, no toil, no sacrifices, to save his country, and to raise his children to a condition better than his own, may my name and the name of my posterity be blotted forever from the memory of mankind."

These passages are not of the best of Mr. Webster's literary efforts, but they show the nature and depth of his attachment to his family and his country.

In respect to Mr. Webster's powers of argument as a close technical lawyer, he may be read at his best in the case of Ogden and Saunders.

Although the question was a constitutional question, the argument was within narrow limits. The Supreme Court had already decided that it was not competent for a State to pass a bankrupt law by which debtors should be discharged from pre-existing contracts.

In the case of Ogden and Saunders, the court was called to decide whether a State could pass an act by which debtors could be relieved from contracts made subsequent to the date of the law.

With great ingenuity of reasoning Mr. Webster contended that a State had no more power to impair a future contract than it had to impair a prior contract. The court, by a majority, held that the obligation of a contract made subsequent to the passage of the bankrupt law, was not impaired by a provision that the obligor might be discharged from his obligation, although he had not performed it. Chief-Justice Marshall and Justices Darrall and Story dissented. In support of this doctrine, finally accepted by the majority of the court, it was argued at the bar that, upon the passage of a bankrupt law by a State, the statute was imported into and became a part of all subsequent contracts.

This theory was assailed by Mr. Webster in an unanswerable argument, but the court appears to have accepted the theory in substance, if not in terms. The leading opinion by the majority was given by Mr. Justice Washington, and he relied upon a technical distinction between a contract and the obligation of a contract.

He maintained that the contract was the work of the parties, but that the obligation of a contract was the creature of the law. This is an error both in law and ethics. The obligation of a contract is what is declared to be the mind of the parties as it is expressed in the contract.

It is the province of the law to find, by judicial processes, the nature and extent of the obligation assumed by the parties, and then to enforce the performance of the obligation. The law creates nothing. It has no power to create either the obligation or the contract.

Possibly the error of the court may be found in the original opinion, Sturgis *vs.* Crowninshield. In that case it was held that a State might pass a bankrupt law, subject to the condition that existing contracts could not be affected.

The Constitution gave to Congress power to pass a *uniform* system of bankruptcy; and it also provided that a State should not pass any law impairing the obligation of contracts.

As these provisions are of the same instrument, they should have been considered together, and a conclusion should have been reached which was reasonable and which would also give effect to the language employed. The court might have said that the grant of power to Congress to establish a uniform system of bankruptcy was equivalent to the denial of the power to the States to establish a State system. This construction was open to two objections, one of public convenience and the other of constitutional interpretation.

If Congress should neglect to enact and maintain a uniform system of bankruptcy, as, in fact, it has neglected to enact and maintain such a system for much the larger part of our national existence, the denial of any power to the States would have resulted in a serious and irremediable inconvenience. And next, inasmuch as the Constitution contains many inhibitions upon the powers of the States, and as the power to pass bankrupt acts is not among them, there was no tenable ground on which the court could add to the disabilities of the States.

The power of the court was thus limited to a definition of the bankrupt law which a State might pass. In the nature of our system there was one limitation to the powers of the States. A State bankrupt law could not be uniform inasmuch as the jurisdiction of a State is limited to its own citizens and to contracts made under its laws.

It might therefore with reason have been held that the power granted by Congress to establish a *uniform* system of bankruptcy was designed to supplement the power reserved to the States.

Again, it is not unreasonable to assume that the right of a State to enact a bankrupt law is the same in its nature and quality as the power granted to Congress, subject only to the necessary limitation that it can not be uniform.

There are also two other considerations leading to the same conclusion. In England, and in the States under the Confederation, it was a recognized power of a government to relieve a debtor from his debts under a bankrupt system. It is also to be observed that, by virtue of each of the three bankrupt laws of the United States, the power to grant to debtors a full and free discharge from all their debts and obligations has been conferred upon the courts. In presence of these authorities, and upon a fair construction of the Constitution, the Supreme Court might have held that the grant of power to Congress was supplementary of the power existing in the States, and that a bankrupt law enacted by a State could operate upon its citizens as a bankrupt law enacted by Congress could operate upon the citizens of the United States.

A system of bankruptcy has an adequate foundation in public morals. A government should not require its citizens or subjects to attempt impossibilities. It must happen often that men engaged in large undertakings become insolvent, and under such circumstances that it is practically impossible for them to meet their liabilities in full either in the present or the future.

In such a condition it is against public policy to hold such persons in semi-servitude. Their abilities and services have a value not to themselves merely, put to the public also.

In the case of Sturgis *vs.* Crowninshield (4 Wheaton, 122), the court held that a State bankrupt law which provided for the discharge of the debtor from the obligation of a contract existing at the time the statute was enacted, was unconstitutional, and upon the ground that it was a violation of the provision which denies to States the power to pass any law impairing the obligation of contracts.

In the case of Ogden and Saunders the court was called to decide the question, Can a State, by virtue of a bankrupt law, relieve a debtor from the obligation of a contract made subsequent to the passage of the law?

It seems an absurdity to maintain that the existing laws in regard to the enforcement of contracts are incorporated into every contract between individuals ; but in the case of Ogden and Saunders the court was driven to that conclusion, in substance, and the theory was announced in the opinion of Mr. Justice Washington. Mr. Webster combated that view, and he was sustained by Chief-Justice Marshall.

A law speaks in the present tense, and it does not speak until there is a case. Manifestly the obligation of a contract does not arise from the statute, but from the intent of the parties of which the contract is the evidence. Consequently, the obligation is the same when there is a bankrupt law in force as when there is no such law; and consequently, also, a law which sets aside or annuls or qualifies the obligation, necessarily impairs that obligation, and that without reference to the condition of the law when the contract was made. Otherwise parties and the court would search the statutes for the nature of a contract obligation instead of examining the contract itself. It might have been a reasonable construction for the court to have held that contracts, which in their nature and by usage, were subject to the operation of a bankrupt law were excepted out of the inhibition to States in regard to contracts.

It is a noticeable feature of Mr. Webster's career that two of his most important forensic efforts were made in criminal causes, one for the defense and one for the prosecution.

In 1817 he defended two young men named Kenniston, who were charged with assaulting and robbing one Goodridge upon the highway between the town of Exeter, in the State of New Hampshire, and Newburyport, Massachusetts. Goodridge was wounded in the hand by a pistol-shot, and he claimed that a considerable sum of money had been taken from him. By Mr. Webster's skill he was at once put upon the defensive. Persons charged with crimes of the nature of robbery, arson, or murder, are usually driven to account for their existence and doings at the time when the crime was committed. Goodridge was called to stand a similar test. He was four or four and a half hours on the way from Exeter to Newburyport, when he could have driven over the road in two or two and a half hours. This delay Goodridge was unable to explain. It was shown that money and papers were found in the house occupied by the accused, but only in places to which Goodridge had had access.

The verdict by which the accused were acquitted was received by the public as a verdict of guilty against Goodridge.

At the trial of the Knapps, in 1830, Mr. Webster, who appeared in behalf of the government, had occasion to refer to the Goodridge case. In that case, Judge William Prescott, father of the historian, was retained by the government to aid in the prosecution. When Mr. Webster appeared for

the government at the trial of the Knapps, the
counsel for the accused complained of his presence,
and said that he had been brought there to hurry
the court and jury "against the law and beyond
the evidence." In his long career at the bar, in
Congress, and in general politics, he never allowed
a personal imputation to rest for a day without reply and rebuke. He asserted himself in his reply
to Hayne, in his defense against the attacks of
Ingersoll, in his scornful denunciation of the reso-
lutions of the Whig party of Massachusetts in 1842,
and in his many letters and speeches in justifica-
tion of his speech of the 7th of March, 1850.

In reply to the aspersions cast upon him by the
counsel for the Knapps, he indulged in deferential
compliments to the court, assuring the members
that if he made the attempt it would be impossible
to carry them against the law; and to the jury he
said that they could "not be hurried beyond the
evidence." Turning to the counsel for the prisoners, and referring to the Goodridge robbery, he
said :

" I remember that the learned head of the Suf-
folk bar, Mr. Prescott, came down in aid of the
officers of the government. This was regarded as
neither strange nor improper. The counsel for the
prisoners, in that case, contented themselves with
answering his arguments, as far as they were able,
instead of carping at his presence."

The murder of Captain White was committed by Richard Crowninshield, for a sum of money to be paid by Joseph J. Knapp, Jr. John Francis Knapp, his brother, was a party to the conspiracy. After the arrest of the parties, Joseph made a full confession to the Rev. Mr. Colman. When Crowninshield heard of the confession, he committed suicide. He had declared previously that he would never submit himself to the degradation of a public execution. It may be true, also, that he thought that by his death his associates might escape conviction upon the charge of murder. As the law then stood, the accessories could not be convicted until after the conviction of the principal. Crowninshield was the principal and the Knapps were accessories. It was proved that Frank Knapp stood at the corner of Brown Street at the time of the murder, and at a point where he had a full view of the house. It was also proved that he met Crowninshield as he came from the house, that they walked together for a time, and that they were together when Crowninshield hid the club, with which he had struck the fatal blow, under the steps of a church.

It was the theory of the government that Frank Knapp was at Brown Street for the purpose of aiding Crowninshield in case of necessity, and upon that theory he was convicted as a principal. The final and more deliberate opinion is that he was not there for any such purpose. In an interview that he had with Crowninshield the preceding afternoon, Crowninshield had said that he did not feel like doing the work that night; and the probability is, that there was no arrangement for aid on the part of Knapp, and that it was only a restless, intense interest in the matter that carried him to a place of observation. Joseph Knapp repudiated his confession, which he had been led to believe would secure a commutation of punishment if not pardon for his crime, and he and his brother were convicted and executed.

The murder of Captain White was a tragedy as horrid as any recorded in play or history; the suicide of Richard Crowninshield was a tragedy with a quality of heroism in it; and there is something which appeals to the better elements of our human nature in the final decision of Joseph Knapp, in refusing to save himself at the sacrifice of his brother's life.

It is not an easy task to select one from Mr. Webster's many speeches, and with confidence assign pre-eminence to that one. With hesitation I give the first place to his argument in the trial of Frank Knapp. It presents six great features. First of all, his description of the murder scene. Next, his essay on the secret, which he closes in

these words : " It must be confessed, it will be confessed ; there is no refuge from confession but suicide, and suicide is confession." Then came his
analysis of the evidence, which could not have
been surpassed by Mr. Choate, who was the un-
rivaled master of that branch of the profession.
Then we have his summary of the evidence which
he marshaled as the equivalent of the confession of
Joseph, as it had been related by Mr. Colman, but
which was of doubtful competency :

" Compare what you learn from this confession
with what you before knew.
" As to its being proposed by Joseph, was not
that before known ?
" As to Richard being in the house alone, was
not that known?
" As to the daggers, was not that known ?
" As to the time of the murder, was not that
known?
" As to his being out that night, was not that
known?
" As to his returning afterward, was not that
known?
" As to the club, was not that known ? "

Then came his summary in propositions as de-
duced from the mass of evidence :

" Gentlemen, I think you can not doubt there
was a conspiracy formed for the purpose of com-
6

mitting this murder, and who the conspirators were.

" That you can not doubt that the Crownin-shields and the Knapps were the parties in this con-spiracy.

" That you can not doubt that the prisoner at the bar knew that the murder was to be done on the night of the 6th of April.

" That you can not doubt that the murderers of Captain White were the suspicious persons seen in and about Brown Street on that night.

" That you can not doubt that Richard Crown-inshield was the perpetrator of that crime.

" That you can not doubt that the prisoner at the bar was in Brown Street on that night.

" If there, then it must be by agreement, to countenance, to aid the perpetrator. And if so, then he is guilty as principal."

He then gave to the jury some solemn admo-nitions as to the obligations resting upon them. Among other observations, was this:

" There is no evil that we can not either face or fly from, but the consciousness of duty disregarded. A sense of duty pursues us ever. It is omnipres-ent, like the Deity."

The number of speeches that are equally sus-tained in all their parts is not large. The argu-ment in the Knapp trial is an exception in that re-spect to speeches generally and to Mr. Webster's especially.

In most of Mr. Webster's arguments and orations there are spaces which are uninteresting to the reader, and in their delivery they were uninteresting to the hearer. Indeed, Mr. Webster was accustomed to pass over portions of his addresses as if they were of very trifling consequence. In the Knapp trial his whole nature was alive. The deed was a horrible one; the public excitement was intense; the circumstances connected with the discovery of the criminals were extraordinary; and, finally, the name of a person, with whom Mr. Webster's family had relations had been mentioned in connection with the crime.

These facts, one and all, tended to produce in Mr. Webster's mind a fixed purpose to secure the conviction of the real criminals.

Mr. Webster's intellectual power was so great that he dominated over ordinary men, and juries were often unable to avoid the conclusions to which he invited them.

In 1821 he was retained to defend Judge Prescott before the Massachusetts Senate, upon articles of impeachment preferred by the House of Representatives.

Much of his argument is devoted to an examination of the evidence which related to fees and extra sessions of the court held by the request and at the cost of suitors.

The prosecution had its origin in personal hostility and political feeling. Prescott was convicted,
and upon proofs which the Senate could not disre-
gard ; but the proofs related to a state of facts
which the House of Representatives might have
passed over without formal notice. Mr. Webster's
closing appeal to the Senate is embraced within
the limits of twelve or fifteen hundred words, and
it is a rare specimen of ethical, special pleading.
It was without influence with the Senate, but it
might have been effectual if it had been addressed
to a jury.

For twenty years Mr. Webster was the recognized head of the American bar, and yet he was
not a learned man, nor a lawyer of long-continued
experience in the profession. He was admitted to
practice in 1805, and in 1812 he was elected to
Congress. From that time onward his professional
career was broken and unsystematic. His pre-
eminence was due to his intellectual supremacy,
and to the adaptation of his faculties to a pursuit
which finds its strongest support in the experience
of ages and the purest human reason.

The learning that is essential to the lawyer may
be, and usually it is, useful to the statesman. It is
also true that the practice of the profession in its
higher departments is a fit preparation for successful work in the field of statesmanship. Previous to

the year 1830, when Mr. Webster made his speech
in reply to Hayne, he had served six years in Congress; he had been a leading member of the Massachusetts Constitutional Convention of 1820; he had
discussed important questions of constitutional law
before the Supreme Court of the United States;
and in every place and upon all questions he had
shown overmastering ability; but the support
which he then gave to General Jackson, in his effort
to suppress nullification, placed him at once and
without debate in the first class of American statesmen. From that time onward, until the day of his
death, his only rivals were Clay and Calhoun.
They were rivals in the opinion of the masses, but
neither of them was his equal in intellectual power.
And, aside from this consideration, the claim to
statesmanship can not be made for Mr. Calhoun.
He identified himself with the institution of slavery, and, subsequent to the close of the war with
Great Britain, his policy never comprehended the
whole country. To the section and to the interest
that he represented he left a legacy of individual
and public suffering such as has not fallen to the
lot of any people since the early Christians were
hidden in the Catacombs or slaughtered in the
amphitheatre of ancient Rome.

The gift of statesmanship and the power of the
statesman can not be denied to Mr. Clay. He was

an early and, in the main, a consistent advocate
of the system of protection to American industry; he supported a national bank; he favored
a plan of internal improvements, and the improvement of the rivers and harbors of the country, at
the public expense. All these measures have, in
principle, been accepted by the country. His
policy is sustained by one of the great parties, and
it receives a partial or qualified support from the
other great party. It is, however, a singular com-
ment upon Mr. Clay's influence that the State which
he represented in the House, in the Senate, in the
Cabinet, and upon a foreign mission, gives no support to the great measures with which he was identified during the whole of his public life. Mr.
Clay's policy survives in that section of the country
to which he did not belong and which he did not
represent.

Mr. Webster was known as the defender of the
Constitution; and that he was, for he well knew
that the Union would stand as long as the Constitution was observed. The Union was the main
thought of his speech in reply to Hayne, and he
never failed to return to that thought in all his subsequent addresses.

Calhoun's teachings tended to the destruction
of the Union; Webster's teachings tended to its
preservation.

Upon Calhoun, more than upon any other man, rests the responsibility for the civil war. Mr. Webster strove to avert the evils of war, and, although his efforts were in vain, yet his speeches, and especially his speech of 1830, educated a generation of men in the free States to the duty of maintaining the Constitution and the Union under it.

In political sentiment the armies of the South represented Mr. Calhoun, and the armies of the North represented Mr. Webster. It is no doubt true, as to the North, that the physical facts were such that the scheme of the South would have been resisted if Mr. Webster had never spoken; but it is equally true that Mr. Webster infused his spirit of attachment to the Union into the whole body of thinkers and readers in the Northern section of the country.

When Mr. Webster made his speech of the 7th of March, 1850, he was far along in the sixty-eighth year of his age. He was a candidate for the presidency. His motives may not have been clear, even to himself. Ambition and a sense of duty may have been so blended that he did not realize how far his sense of duty was controlled by his wish to conciliate interests that theretofore had been hostile. As there were bodies of intelligent, patriotic persons in the North who shared his apprehensions and who supported his policy, it is reasonable to assume that Mr. Webster acted upon his judgment, and without reference to personal considerations.

The settlement of the northeastern boundary dispute, in 1842, was Mr. Webster's work. It was stated by Mr. Webster, in substance, that the President left the business to him, and it is neither unreasonable nor unjust to assume that Mr. Tyler was wholly indifferent to the question of territory, which was the real difficulty in the negotiations. As to Mr. Webster, he had to negotiate with three parties—Great Britain, Maine, and Massachusetts. Maine claimed jurisdiction, and Maine and Massachusetts claimed property in the lands, some of which were ceded to Great Britain.

It can not be said of Mr. Webster that he originated any important public policy, but in ability to maintain a policy that he had embraced he was far superior to his Whig associates. Mr. Webster was a conservative by nature, and hence it came to pass that he opposed the system of protection when commerce was the chief interest of New England ; and hence it was that he defended the system of protection when, by the policy of the Government, the capital of New England had been invested in manufactures. He had no respect for the claim that political economy is a cosmopolitan science, and hence he favored such legislation as promised the best results to the people of the United States. In that he did not err. The maxim, "Buy where you can buy cheapest and sell where you can sell dearest," is often a fallacy as a measure of public policy. It is the duty of a government to favor that public policy which will secure to the laborer for each day's labor the largest return in the necessaries, conveniences, and comforts of personal and family life. This the policy of protection has done. If we compare the laboring-classes, in their condition, since 1861, with their condition during the previous sixty years, we shall find that there has been a continuous improvement. It can be said, also, that the laboring-classes of Europe have advanced in the last twenty-five years. The remark is true ; but the value of the remark is qualified by the fact that the improvement in Europe has been much less than in America, and by the important circumstances that the higher wages and better condition of American laborers have drawn to America large classes of farmers and artisans, thereby improving the condition of those who remained at home.

In diplomatic debate Mr. Webster has not been surpassed by any one who has held the office of Secretary of State, but the questions that he was called to consider were much inferior in importance to those which subsequently engaged the attention of Mr. Seward and Mr. Fish.

Mr. Webster had a successful career, although, in his ambition to become President, he was disappointed. Such failures have been frequent; and as the attainment of the office is not in all cases a success, so the failure to attain it is not in all cases a misfortune. He was at once the head of the American bar, the first English-speaking orator when his powers were at their maturity, and a recognized master in the list of American statesmen.

Mr. Webster was one of the last of a long line of American statesmen who, in the presence of slavery, strove to preserve liberty and the Union, and of that long line he was the greatest. For seventy years the thoughtful men of all parties were forced to consider the system of slavery in America, its relations to the Union, and its inherent antagonism to the principles on which the Government was founded. Of all Mr. Webster's contemporaries no one was more susceptible than he to these influences. By nature, by education, and upon his mature judgment, he was opposed to every form of human servitude. In 1820 he anathematized slavery in invectives fierce and strong as any which ever fell from the lips of Clarkson, Wilberforce, Phillips, or Garrison.

No martyr was ever more devoted to his faith than was Mr. Webster to the Union of the States, and to its service he had contributed the best thoughts of his life and the most brilliant passages of his orations. There can be no reasonable doubt that in 1850, to Mr. Webster's eye, the ways seemed to part. He thought that the Union was in peril, and that the further agitation of the slavery question would add to the peril.

Slavery had given birth to one form of civilization, and freedom had given birth to another, and from the beginning the rule of the continent was the prize for which the parties had contended. Each succeeding census made clear and more clear the truth that time was on the side of liberty, and that a postponement of the struggle would be fatal to slavery. Hence each census from 1820 to 1860, inclusive, with the exception of that of 1840, when the public mind was preoccupied with grave questions of finance, wrought a crisis which menaced the public peace. On two occasions Mr. Webster met the peril and controlled it : First, in 1830, when he chose his place with General Jackson, and won imperishable fame on the floor of the Senate ; and again in 1850, when he secured a postponement of the contest, but at the sacrifice of his popularity and the ruin of his political fortunes.

Mr. Webster claimed that the postponement of

the struggle would result in the supremacy of
liberty and the preservation of the Union; and
it would be unjust to deny to him that foresight,
statesmanship, and patriotism which the claim in-
volves. It is true, indeed, that he did not anticipate the immediate abolition of slavery. His
thoughts and policy contemplated only peaceful
measures—first, the limitation of the system, and
then the gradual emancipation of the slaves.

The compromise measures of 1850 gave the
North ten years of time, and those years were
years of preparation for the struggle of 1860 and
the war of the rebellion.

In these ten years the public mind was educated and the body of the people were prepared
for the solution of the problem, whether by peace
or war. If the contest had been precipitated in
1850, the result might have been a division of the
republic, and for the continent there would have
been neither union nor liberty.

It is not just to Mr. Webster to assume that he
builded better than he knew. He builded as he
knew.

At the moment of his death his policy appeared
to be acceptable to the country; but, in less than
two years, old compromises were violated, and it
was then idle and in vain to make appeals in behalf of the new. In the review we must admit

that the processes of compromise from the formation of the Constitution to the opening of the rebellion were calculated to preserve liberty and the Union, and, in the end, to render them one and inseparable.

The incidental results were disagreeable, but they were also temporary. The end was freedom for the continent, and a continent included within the limits of the Union. Thus liberty and the Union became one and inseparable.

For twenty years Mr. Webster was the chief personage in Massachusetts, in New England, in the republic. In politics he had competitors; but in diplomacy, in logical precision and force, in knowledge of the Constitution, in ability to deal with the gravest questions of law and statesmanship, in that genius by whose power he adorned whatever he said with an imagery as bold and magnificent as that of Milton and as true to nature as that of Shakespeare, he was without an equal or a rival. Wherever he stood, he was great; and the demand which he made for public consideration was based on that greatness.

Mr. Webster was not an unconscious bearer of a royal intellect, and at the end he was forced to look with something of contempt upon that public sentiment which advanced inferior men and denied to him the chiefest honor of the republic.

When Mr. Webster spoke at Plymouth in 1820, when he spoke in the Senate of 1830, there were men living who had heard Burke, and Fox, and Sheridan ; and with them only, of all English-speaking orators, was he contrasted or compared. And if, for the moment, we can command the whole range of history, it is difficult to summon another orator who, in the Senate, and in the contest of 1830, could have met so completely the demand of the occasion, and justified his cause and the conduct of it to future ages. And if, again, for the moment we can command the whole range of history, can its ten great orators be named, and Mr. Webster be excluded from the list? Of those who have spoken the English language, he is inferior only to Burke ; and if the position which Macaulay assigns to Burke shall be sustained by the continuing judgment of mankind, then will Mr. Webster's countrymen claim for him the second place on the page of universal history.

An orator is not made by a single happy paragraph, nor born of one fortunate speech. He is to live in the public eye through a long period of time, and he must deal temperately, forcibly, persuasively, wisely, with a variety of questions touching the public interests or relating to the public welfare. All these conditions, and whatever else may be demanded of the orator, were fully met in Mr. Webster's career.

Mr. Webster was great in intellect, majestic in his person, great in his friendships, great in his enmities.

His fame rests upon the intellectual forces that he possessed, and the nature and extent of the uses to which they were applied. A public man can not choose his career. He must deal with the questions of his own generation. It was Mr. Webster's fortune to be called to the study and discussion of a new Constitution framed for a new people. In the main his views have been sustained by judicial decisions and sanctioned by the course of political events.

The virtue of a written constitution is in the interpretation given to it. Mr. Webster spoke for national life, for national power, for public honor, for public virtue.

His views of the Constitution are to be considered by all who shall study that Constitution and by all who are called to interpret it. He has thus become a worker in all the future of the republic.

The two great orators of antiquity pleaded the cause of dying states, but it was Mr. Webster's better fortune to aid in giving form and character to a young and growing nation.

PRESIDENT LINCOLN.

WHEN Anson Burlingame was in this country the last time, he gave me an account of his life in China, his relations with the principal personages there, and said, finally: " When I die they will erect monuments and temples to my memory. However much I may now protest, they will do that." This, we are told, the people and Government of China have done.

Gratitude to public benefactors is the common sentiment of mankind. It has found expression in every age; it finds expression in every condition of society. Monuments and temples seem to belong to the age of art rather than to the age of letters; but reflection teaches us that letters can not fully express the obligations of the learned even, to their chief benefactors, and only in a less degree can epitaphs, essays, and histories satisfy those who have not the opportunity and culture to read and understand them. Moreover, monuments and temples in honor of the dead express the sentiments of their contemporaries who survive; and the sentiments of contemporaries, when freed from passion, crystallize, usually, into opinion —the fixed, continuing opinion of mankind. Napoleon must ever remain great; Washington, good and great; Burke, the first of English orators; the younger Pitt, the chief of English statesmen; and Henry VIII, a dark character in British history. Time and reflection, the competing fame of new and illustrious men, the antiquarian and the critic, may modify the first-formed opinion, but seldom or never is it changed. The judgment rendered at the grave is a just judgment usually, but whether so or not it is not often disturbed.

The fame of noble men is at once the most enduring and the most valuable public possession. Of the distant past it is all of value that remains; and of the recent past, the verdant fields, the villages, cities, and institutions of culture and government are only monuments which men of that past have reared to their own fame. History is but the account of men: the earth, even, is but a mighty theatre on which human actors, great and small, have played their parts.

Superior talents and favoring circumstances have secured for a few persons that special recognition called immortality; that is, a knowledge of qualities and actions attributed to an individual

7

whose name is preserved and transmitted, with that knowledge, from one generation to another. This immortality may be nothing to the dead, but the record furnishes examples and inspiring facts, especially for the young, by which they are encouraged and stimulated to lead lives worthy of the illustrious men of the past. Herein is the value, and the chief value, of monuments, temples, histories, and panegyrics. If the highest use of sinners is, by their evil lives and bad examples, to keep saints to their duty, so it is also that the immortality accorded to those who were scourges rather than benefactors serves as a warning to men who strive to write their names upon the page of history. But the world really cherishes only the memory of those who were good as well as great, and hence it is the effort of panegyrists and hero-worshipers to place their idols in that attitude before mankind. The immortal few are those who have identified themselves with contests and principles in which men of all times are interested; or who have so expressed the wish or thought or purpose of mankind that their words both enlighten and satisfy the thoughtful of every age. When we consider how much is demanded of aspirants for lasting fame, we can understand the statement that that century is rich which adds more than one name to the short list of persons who, in an historical sense, are immortal. In that sense those only are immortal whose fame passes beyond the country, beyond the race, beyond the language, beyond the century, and far outspreads all knowledge of the details of local and national history.

The empire of Japan sent accredited to the United States, as its first minister resident, Ari Nori Mori, a young man of extraordinary ability, and then only twenty-four years of age. A few months before Japan was opened to intercourse with other nations, an elder brother of Mori lived for a time as a student at Jeddo, the capital of the empire. Upon his return to his home in the country he informed the family that he had heard of a new and distant nation of which Washington, the greatest and best of men, was the founder, savior, and father. Beyond this he had heard little of the country or the man, but this brief statement so inspired the younger brother to know more of the man and of the country, that he re-solved to leave his native land without delay, and in disobedience both to parental rule and public law. In this single fact we see what fame is in its largest sense, and we realize also the power of a single character to influence others, even where there is no tie of country, of language, of race, or any except that which gives unity to the

whole family of man. If, then, the acquisition of
fame in a large sense be so difficult, is it wise
thus to present the subject to the young? May
they not be deterred from those manly efforts
which are the prerequisites of success? I answer,
Fame is not a proper object of human effort, and
its pursuit is the most unwise of human undertakings. I am not now moralizing; I am trying
to state the account as a worldly transaction.
Moreover, there is a distinction between the fame
of which I have spoken and contemporaneous
recognition of one's capacity and fitness to perform important private or public service. This
is reputation rather than fame, and it may well
. be sought by honorable effort, and it should be
prized by every one as an object of virtuous ambition. Success, however, is not so often gained
by direct effort as by careful, systematic, thorough
preparation for duty. The world is not so loaded
with genius, nor even with talent, that opportunities are wanting for all those who have capacity
for public service.

Mr. Bancroft gave voice to the considerate
judgment of mankind when, in conversation, he
said, " Beyond question, General Washington, intellectually, is the first of Americans." If this
statement be open to question, the question springs
from the limitation, for beyond doubt Washington

is the first of Americans. His pre-eminence, his greatness, appear in the fact that his faculties and powers were so fully developed, so evenly adjusted and nicely balanced that, in all the various and difficult duties of military and civil life, he never for an instant failed to meet the demand which his position and the attendant circumstances made upon him. This was the opinion of his contemporaries. His pre-eminence was felt and recognized by the leaders of the savage tribes of America, by the most sagacious statesmen and wisest observers in foreign lands, and by all of his countrymen who were able to escape the influence of passion and to consider passing events in the light of pure reason.

It is the glory of Washington that he was the first great military chief who did not exhibit the military spirit; and in this he has given to his country an example and a rule of the highest value. The problem of republics is to develop military capacity without fostering the military spirit. This Washington did in himself, and this also his country has done. The zeal of the young men of the republic to enter the military service for the defense of the Union, and the satisfaction with which they accepted peace and returned to the employments of peace, all in obedience to the example of Washington, are his highest praise.

Washington was also an illustration of the axiom in government that the faculties and qualities essential to a military leader are the highest endowments of a ruler in time of peace; and the instincts of men are in harmony with this historic and philosophic truth. The time that has passed since the public career and natural life of Washington ended has not dimmed the luster of his fame, nor qualified in the least that general judgment on which he was raised to an equality with the most renowned personages of ancient and modern times.

With this estimate, not an unusual nor an exaggerated estimate, I venture to claim for Abraham Lincoln the place next to Washington, whether we have regard to private character, to intellectual qualities, to public services, or to the weight of obligation laid upon the country and upon mankind. Between Washington and Lincoln there were two full generations of men; but, of them all, I see not one who can be compared with either.

Submitting this opinion in advance of all evidence, I proceed to deal with those qualities, opportunities, characteristics, and services on which Lincoln's claim rests for the broad and most enduring fame of which I have spoken. We are attracted naturally by the career of a man who

THE STATESMAN AND LIBERATOR.

has passed from the humblest condition in early
life to stations of honor and fame in maturer years.
With Lincoln this space was the broadest possible
in civilized life.   His childhood was spent in a
cabin upon a mud floor, and his youth and early
manhood were checkered with more than the usual
share of vicissitudes and disappointments.   The
chief blessing of his early life was his step-mother,
Sally Bush, who, by her affectionate treatment and
wise conduct, did much to elevate the character
of the class of women to which she belonged.   His
opportunities for training in the schools were few,
and his hours of study were limited.   The books
that he could obtain were read and re-read, and a
grammar and geometry were his constant companions for a time; but his means of education
bore no logical relation to the position he finally
reached as a thinker, writer, and speaker.   Lincoln
is a witness for the man William Shakespeare
against those hostile and illogical critics who deny
to him the authorship of the plays that bear his
name, because they can not comprehend the way
of reaching such results without the aid of books,
teachers, and universities.   When they show similar results reached by the aid of books, teachers,
and universities, or even by their aid chiefly, they
will then have one fact tending to prove that
such results can not be reached without such

aids; but in the absence of the proof we must
accept Shakespeare and Lincoln, and confess our
ignorance of the processes by which their greatness was attained.

·Books, schools, and universities are helps to
all, and they are needed by each and all in the
ratio of the absence of natural capacity. By the
processes of reason employed to show that Shakespeare did not write "Hamlet," it may be proved
that Lincoln did not compose the speech which
he pronounced at Gettysburg. The parallel between Shakespeare·and Lincoln is good to this
extent. The products of the pen of Lincoln imply a degree of culture in schools which he never
had, and a process of reasoning upon that impli-
cation leads to the conclusion that he was not
the author of what bears his name. We know
that this conclusion would be false, and we may
therefore question the soundness of a similar process of reasoning in the case of Shakespeare.

The world gives too much credit to self-made
men. Not much is due to those who are so
largely endowed by Nature that they at once
outrun their contemporaries who are always on
the crutches of books and authorities, and but a
little more is due to the larger class who, in iso-
lation and privation, acquire the knowledge that
is gained, usually, only in the schools. In the

end, however, we judge the man as a whole and
as a result, for there is no trustworthy analysis
by which we can decide how much is due to
Nature, how much to personal effort, and how
much to circumstances. Of all the self-made men
of America, Lincoln owed least to books, schools,
and society. Washington owed much to these,
and all his self-assertion, which was considerable,
in society, in the army, and in civil affairs, was
the assertion of a trained man. Lincoln asserted
nothing but his capacity, when it was his duty, to
decide what was wise and what was right. He
claimed nothing for himself, in his personal character, in the nature of deference from others, and
too little, perhaps, for the great office he held.
The schools create nothing ; they only bring out
what is ; but, as long as the mass of mankind
think otherwise, an untrained person like Lincoln
has an immense advantage over the scholar in
the contest for immortality. In this particular,
however, the instincts of men have a large share
of wisdom in them. When we speak of human
greatness we mean natural, innate faculty and
power. We distinguish the gift of God from the
culture of the schools. The unlearned give the
schools too much credit in the work of developing
power and forming character ; the learned, perhaps, give them too little. But, whether judged

by the learned or the unlearned, Lincoln is the most commanding figure in the ranks of self-made men which America has yet produced.

Mr. Lincoln possessed the almost divine faculty of interpreting the will of the people without any expression by them. We often hear of the influence of the atmosphere of Washington upon the public men residing there. It never affected him. He was of all men most independent of locality and social influences. He was wholly self-contained in all that concerned his opinions upon public questions and in all his judgments of the popular will. Conditions being given, he could anticipate the popular will and conduct. When the proceedings of the convention of dissenting Republicans, which assembled at Cleveland in 1864, were mentioned to him and his opinion sought, he told the story of two fresh Irishmen who attempted to find a tree-toad that they heard in the forest, and how, after a fruitless hunt, one of them consoled himself and his companion with the expression, "An' faith it was nothing but a noise."

Mr. Lincoln's goodness of nature was boundless. In childhood it showed itself in unfeigned aversion to every form of cruelty to animal life. When he was President it found expression in that memorable letter to Mrs. Bixby, of Boston, who had given, irrevocably given, as was then supposed, five sons to the country. The letter was dated November 21, 1864, before the excitement of his second election was over:

"DEAR MADAM : I have been shown, in the files of the War Department, a statement, of the Adjutant-General of Massachusetts, that you are the mother of five sons who have died gloriously on the field of battle. I feel how weak and fruitless must be any words of mine which should attempt to beguile you from a loss so overwhelming. But I can not refrain from tendering to you the consolation that may be found in the thanks of the republic they died to save. I pray that our heavenly Father may assuage the anguish of your bereavement, and leave you only the cherished memory of the loved and lost, and the solemn pride that must be yours to have laid so costly a sacrifice upon the altar of freedom.

"Yours, very sincerely and respectfully,

"ABRAHAM LINCOLN.

"To Mrs. Bixby, Boston, Massachusetts."

I imagine that all history and all literature may be searched, and in vain, for a funereal tribute so touching, so comprehensive, so fortunate in expression as this.

If we have been moved to laughter by a sim-

ple story, and to tears by a pathetic strain, we
can understand what Lincoln was to all, and especially to the common people who were his fellows
in everything except his greatness, when he moved,
spoke, and acted among them. It would be a
reflection upon the human race if men did not
recognize something worthy of enduring fame in
one whose kindness and sympathy were so comprehensive as to include the insect on the one
side and the noble, but bereaved, mother on the
other. To the soldiers, General Thomas was "Old
Holdfast," General Hooker was "Fighting Joe,"
and Mr. Lincoln was "Father Abraham." These
names were due to personal qualities which the
soldiers observed, admired, and applauded.

Mr. Lincoln was a mirth-making, genial, melancholy man. By these characteristics he enlisted
sympathy for himself at once, while his moral
qualities and intellectual pre-eminence commanded
respect. Mr. Lincoln's wit and mirth will give him
a passport to the thoughts and hearts of millions
who would take no interest in the sterner and
more practical parts of his character. He used
his faculties for mirth and wit to relieve the melancholy of his life, to parry unwelcome inquiries,
and, in the debates of politics and the bar, to
worry his opponents. In debate he often so combined wit, satire, and statement, that his opponent

at once appeared ridiculous and illogical. Mr. Douglas was often the victim of these sallies in the great debate for the Senate before the people of Illinois, and before the people of the country, in the year 1858. Douglas constantly asserted that abolition would be followed by amalgamation, and that the Republican party designed to repeal the laws of Illinois which prohibited the marriage of blacks and whites. This was a formidable appeal, to the prejudices of the people of Southern Illinois especially. " I protest now and forever," said Lincoln, " against that counterfeit logic which presumes that because I did not want a negro woman for a slave, I do, necessarily, want her for a wife. I have never had the least apprehension that I or my friends would marry negroes if there were no law to keep them from it; but, as Judge Douglas and his friends seem to be in great apprehension that they might, if there were no law to keep them from it, I give him the most solemn pledge that I will, to the very last, stand by the law of this State, which forbids the marrying of white people with negroes." Thus, in two sentences, did Mr. Lincoln overthrow Douglas in his logic, and render him ridiculous in his position.

Douglas claimed special credit for the defeat of the Lecompton bill, although five sixths of the

votes were given by the Republican party. Said
Lincoln: "Why is he entitled to more credit than
others for the performance of that good act, unless
there was something in the antecedents of the Republicans that might induce every one to expect
them to join in that good work, and, at the same
time, leading them to doubt that he would? Does
he place his superior claim to credit on the ground
that he performed a good act which was never
expected of him?" He then gave Mr. Douglas
the benefit of a specific application of the parable
of the lost sheep.

In the last debate at Alton, October 15, 1858,
Mr. Douglas proceeded to show that Buchanan
was guilty of gross inconsistencies of position.
Lincoln did not defend Buchanan, but, after he
had stated the fact that Douglas had been on
both sides of the Missouri Compromise, he added:
"I want to know if Buchanan has not as much
right to be inconsistent as Douglas has? Has
Douglas the exclusive right in this country of
being *on all sides of all questions?* Is nobody allowed that high privilege but himself? Is he to
have an entire monopoly on that subject?"

There are three methods in debate of sustain-
ing and enforcing opinions, and the faculty and
facility of using these several methods are the
tests of intellectual quality in writers and speak-

ers. First, and lowest intellectually, are those who rely upon authority. They gather and marshal the sayings of their predecessors, and ask their hearers and readers to indorse the positions taken, not because they are reasonable and right under the process of demonstration, but because many persons in other times have thought them to be right and reasonable. As this is the work of the mere student, and does not imply either philosophy or the faculty of reasoning, those who rely exclusively upon authority are in the third class of intellectual men. Next, and of a much higher order, are the writers and speakers who state the facts of a case, apply settled principles to them, and by sound processes of reasoning maintain the positions taken. But high above all are the men who, by statement pure and simple, or by statement argumentative, carry conviction to thoughtful minds. Unquestionably Mr. Lincoln belongs to this class. Those who remember Douglas's theory in regard to "squatter sovereignty," which he sometimes dignified by calling it the " sacred right of self-government," will appreciate the force of Lincoln's statement of the scheme in these words: " The phrase, 'sacred right of self-government,' though expressive of the only rightful basis of any government, was so perverted in the attempted use of it as to amount to just this: *That if any one man choose to enslave another, no third man shall be allowed to object."*

In the field of argumentative statement, Mr. Webster, at the time of his death, had had no rival in America; but he has left nothing more exact, explicit, and convincing than this extract from Lincoln's first speech of the great debate. Here is a statement in less than twenty words, *If any one man choose to enslave another, no third man shall be allowed to object,* which embodies the substance of the opinion of the Supreme Court of the United States in the case of Dred Scott, the theory of the Kansas-Nebraska bill, and exposes the sophistry which Douglas had woven into his arguments on " squatter sovereignty."

Douglas constantly appealed to the prejudices of the people, and arrayed them against the doctrine of negro equality. Lincoln, in reply, after asserting their equality under the Declaration of Independence, added, " In the right to eat the bread, without the leave of anybody else, which his own hand earns, he is my equal, and the equal of Judge Douglas, and the equal of every living man." Douglas often said—and he commanded the cheers of his supporters when he said it—" I do not care whether slavery is voted up or voted down." In his final speech at Alton, Lincoln reviewed the history of the churches and of the

Government in connection with slavery, and he then asked: "Is it not a false statesmanship that undertakes to build up a system of policy upon the basis of caring nothing about the very thing that everybody does care the most about?" He then, in the same speech, assailed Douglas's position in an argument, which is but a series of statements, and, as a whole, it is, in its logic and moral sentiment, the equal of anything in the language: "He may say he doesn't care whether an indifferent thing is voted up or down, but he must logically have a choice between a right thing and a wrong thing. He contends that whatever community wants slaves has a right to have them. So they have, if it is not a wrong. But, if it is a wrong, he can not say people have a right to do wrong. He says that, upon the score of equality, slaves should be allowed to go into a new Territory like other property. This is strictly logical, if there is no difference between it and other property. If it and other property are equal, his argument is entirely logical. But, if you insist that one is wrong and the other right, there is no use to institute a comparison between right and wrong. You may turn over everything in the Democratic policy, from beginning to end —whether in the shape it takes on the statute-book, in the shape it takes in the Dred Scott de-

8

cision, in the shape it takes in conversation, or in the shape it takes in short, maxim-like arguments —it everywhere carefully excludes the idea that there is anything wrong in it. That is the real issue. That is the issue that will continue in this country when these poor tongues of Judge Douglas and myself shall be silent. It is the eternal struggle between these two principles, right and wrong, throughout the world. They are the two principles that have stood face to face from the beginning of time, and will ever continue to struggle. The one is the common right of humanity, and the other the divine right of kings. It is the same principle in whatever shape it develops itself. It is the same spirit that says, ‘You work and toil and earn bread, and I'll eat it.’ No matter in what shape it comes, whether from the mouth of a king who seeks to bestride the people of his own nation and live by the fruit of their labor, or from one race of men as an apology for enslaving another race, it is the same tyrannical principle.”

To the Democrat who admitted that slavery was a wrong, Mr. Lincoln addressed himself thus: “You never treat it as a wrong. You must not say anything about it in the free States, because *it is not here*. You must not say anything about it in the slave States, because *it is there*. You

must not say anything about it in the pulpit, because that is religion, and has nothing to do with
it. You must not say anything about it in politics, because that will disturb the security of my
place. There is no place to talk about it as being
wrong, although you say yourself it is a wrong."

Among the rude people with whom Lincoln
passed his youth and early manhood, his personal
courage was often tested, and usually in support
of the rights or pretensions of others, or in behalf
of the weak, the wronged, or the dependent. In
later years his moral characteristics were subjected
to tests equally severe. Mr. Lincoln was not an
agitator like Garrison, Phillips, and O'Connell, and
as a reformer he belonged to the class of moderate men, such as Peel and Gladstone; but in no
condition did he ever confound right with wrong,
or speak of injustice with bated breath. His first
printed paper was a plea for temperance; and his
second, a eulogy upon the Union. His positive,
personal hostility to slavery goes back to the year
1831, when he arrived at New Orleans as a laborer upon a flat-boat. " There it was," says
Hanks, his companion, " we saw negroes chained,
maltreated, whipped, and scourged. Lincoln saw
it, said nothing much, was silent from feeling, was
sad, looked bad, felt bad, was thoughtful and abstracted. I can say, knowing it, that it was on

this trip that he formed his opinion of slavery.
It run its iron in him then and there, May, 1831.
I have heard him say so often and often." In
1850, he said to his partner, Mr. Stuart: "The
time will come when we must all be Democrats
or abolitionists. When that time comes, my mind
is made up. The slavery question can't be com-
promised." In 1855, he said: "Our progress in
degeneracy appears to me to be pretty rapid. As
a nation we began by declaring that *all men are
created equal.* We now practically read it *all men
are created equal except negroes."* In his Ottawa
speech of 1858, he read an extract from his speech
at Peoria, made in 1854, in these words: "This
declared indifference, but as I must think *real* zeal
for the spread of slavery, I can not but hate. I
hate it because of the monstrous injustice of slavery itself. I hate it because it deprives our republican example of its just influence in the world,
enables the enemies of free institutions with plausi-
bility to taunt us as hypocrites, causes the real
friends of freedom to doubt our sincerity, and,
especially, because it forces so many really good
men among ourselves into an open war with the
very fundamental principles of civil liberty, criti-
cising the Declaration of Independence, and in-
sisting that there is no right principle of action
but self-interest."

These extracts prepare the reader for the most important utterance by Mr. Lincoln previous to his elevation to the presidency.

The Republican Convention of the State of Illinois met at Springfield, June 17, 1858, and nominated Mr. Lincoln for the seat in the Senate of the United States then held by Stephen A. Douglas. This action was expected, and Mr. Lincoln had prepared himself to accept the nomination in a speech which he foresaw would be the pivot of the debate with Judge Douglas. That speech he submitted to a council of at least twelve of his personal and political friends, all of whom advised him to omit or to change materially the first paragraph. This Mr. Lincoln refused to do, even when challenged by the opinion that it would cost him his seat in the Senate. It did cost him his seat in the Senate, but the speech would have been delivered had he foreseen that it would cost him much more. After its delivery, and while the canvass was going on, he said to his friends; "You may think that speech was a mistake, but I never have believed it was, and you will see the day when you will consider it was the wisest thing I ever said. If I had to draw a pen across and erase my whole life from existence, and I had one poor gift or choice left as to what I should save from the wreck, I should choose that speech, and leave it to the world un-erased." These are the words that he prized so highly, and which, for the time, cost him so much: " If we could first know where we are and whither we are tending, we could better judge what to do and how to do it. We are now far into the fifth year since a policy was initiated with the avowed object and confident promise of putting an end to slavery agitation. Under the operation of that policy, that agitation has not only not ceased, but has constantly augmented. In my opinion it will not cease until a crisis shall have been reached and passed. 'A house divided against itself can not stand.' I believe this Gov-ernment can not endure permanently, half slave and half free. I do not expect the Union to be dissolved; I do not expect the house to fall; but I do expect it will cease to be divided. It will become all one thing or all the other; either the opponents of slavery will arrest the further spread of it, and place it where the public mind shall rest in the belief that it is in the course of ulti-mate extinction, or its advocates will push it for-ward, till it shall become alike lawful in all the States, old as well as new, North as well as South." To the pro-slavery, sensitive, prejudiced, Union-saving classes it was not difficult to interpret this paragraph in a highly offensive sense. The phrase,

"A house divided against itself can not stand," was interpreted as a declaration against the Union. It was, in fact, a declaration of the existence of the irrepressible conflict.

Douglas availed himself of the opportunity to excite the prejudices of the people, and thus secured his re-election to the Senate. Mr. Lincoln had a higher object: he sought to change public sentiment. No man ever lived who better understood the means of affecting public sentiment, or more highly appreciated its power and importance. At Ottawa he said: "In this and like communities public sentiment is everything. With public sentiment nothing can fail; without it nothing can succeed. Consequently, he who molds public sentiment goes deeper than he who enacts statutes or pronounces decisions. He makes statutes and decisions possible or impossible to be executed."

I have quoted thus freely from Mr. Lincoln, that we may appreciate his moral courage; that we may rest in the opinion that he was an early, constant, consistent advocate of human liberty, and that we might enjoy the charm of his transcendently clear thought, convincing logic, and power of statement. When he became President, and was called to bear the chief burden in the struggle for liberty and the Union, he was never

dismayed by the condition of public affairs, nor
disturbed by apprehensions for his personal safety.
He was like a soldier in the field, enlisted for
duty, and danger was, of course, incident to it.
I was alone with Mr. Lincoln more than two
hours of the Sunday next after Pope's defeat in
August, 1862. That was the darkest day of the
sad years of the war. McClellan had failed upon
the Peninsula. Pope's army, re-enforced by the
remains of the Army of the Peninsula, had been
driven within the fortifications of Washington.
Our losses of men had been enormous, but most
serious of all was the loss of confidence in commanders. The army did not confide in Pope, and
the authorities did not confide in McClellan. In
that crisis Lincoln surrendered his own judgment
to the opinion of the army, and re-established
McClellan in command. When the business to
which I had been summoned by the President
was over—strange business for the time: the appointment of assessors and collectors of internal
revenue—he was kind enough to ask my opinion
as to the command of the army. The way was
thus opened for conversation, and for me to say
at the end that I thought our success depended
upon the emancipation of the slaves. To this he
said: " You would not have it done now, would
you? Must we not wait for something like a

victory?" This was the second and most explicit
intimation to me of his purpose in regard to slavery. In the preceding July or early in August,
at an interview upon business connected with my
official duties, he said, " Let me read two letters,"
and taking them from a pigeon-hole over his table
he proceeded at once to do what he had proposed.
I have not seen the letters in print. His correspondent was a gentleman in Louisiana, who
claimed to be a Union man. He tendered his
advice to the President in regard to the reorganization of that State, and he labored zealously to
impress upon him the dangers and evils of emancipation. The reply of the President is only important from the fact that when he came to that
part of his correspondent's letter he used this expression: " You must not expect me to give up
this Government without playing my last card."
Emancipation was his last card. He waited for
the time when two facts or events should coincide.
Mr. Lincoln was as devoted to the Constitution
as was ever Mr. Webster. In his view, a military
necessity was the only ground on which the overthrow of slavery in the States could be justified.
Next he waited for a public sentiment in the
loyal States not only demanding emancipation but
giving full assurance that the act would be sustained to the end. As for himself, I can not doubt

that he had contemplated the policy of emancipation for many months, and anticipated the
time when he should adopt it. At his interview with the Chicago clergy he stated the reasons against emancipation, and stated them so forcibly that the clergy were not prepared to answer them; but the accredited account of the
interview contains conclusive proof that Mr.
Lincoln then contemplated issuing the proclamation.

It may be remembered by the reader that in
the political campaign of 1862, a prominent leader
of the People's party, the late Judge Joel Parker, of
Cambridge, Massachusetts, said in public that Mr.
Lincoln issued the proclamation under the influence of the loyal Governors who met at Altoona
in September of that year. As I was about to
leave Washington in the month of October to
take part in the canvass, I mentioned to the President the fact that such a statement had been
made. He at once said: "I never thought of the
meeting of the Governors. The truth is just this:
When Lee came over the river, I made a resolution that if McClellan drove him back I would
send the proclamation after him. The battle of
Antietam was fought Wednesday, and until Saturday I could not find out whether we had
gained a victory or lost a battle. It was then too

late to issue the proclamation that day, and the
fact is I fixed it up a little Sunday, and Monday
I let them have it."

Men will probably entertain different opinions
of one part of Lincoln's character. He not only
possessed the apparently innate faculty of com-
prehending the tendency, purposes, and opinions
of masses of men, but he observed and measured
with accuracy the peculiarities of individuals who
were about him, and made those individuals, sometimes through their peculiarities and sometimes in
spite of them, the instruments or agents of his
own views. Of the three chief men in his Cabinet, Seward, Chase, and Stanton, Mr. Stanton was
the only one who never thus yielded to this power
of the President. The reason was creditable alike
to the President and to Mr. Stanton. Mr. Stanton
was frank and fearless in his office, devoted to
duty, destitute of ambition, and uncompromising
in his views touching emancipation and the suppression of the rebellion. The popular sentiment
of the day made no impression upon him. He
was always ready for every forward movement,
and he could never be reconciled to a backward
step, either in the field or the Cabinet. It is no
injustice to Mr. Seward and Mr. Chase to say that
they had ambitions which, under some circumstances, might disturb the judgment. These am-

bitions and their tendencies could not escape the notice of the President.

Mr. Lincoln was indifferent to those matters of government that were relatively unimportant; but he devoted himself with conscientious diligence to the graver questions and topics of official duty, and, in the first months of his administration, at a moment of supreme peril, by his pre-eminent wisdom, of which there remains indubitable proof, he saved the country from a foreign war. I refer to the letter of instruction to Mr. Adams, written in May, 1861, and relating to the proclamation of the Government of Great Britain recognizing the belligerent character of the Confederate States.

In the greatest exigencies his power of judging immediately and wisely did not desert him. On the eve of the battle of Gettysburg, General Hooker resigned the command of the army. This act was a painful, a terrible surprise to Mr. Stanton and the President. Mr. Stanton's account to me was this: "When I received the dispatch my heart sank within me, and I was more depressed than at any other moment of the war. I could not say that any other officer knew General Hooker's plans, or the position even of the various divisions of the army. I sent for the President to come to the War Office at once. It was in the evening, but the President soon appeared. I handed

him the dispatch. As he read it his face became
like lead. I said, 'What shall be done?' He
replied, instantly, 'Accept his resignation.'" In
secret, and without consulting any one else, the
President and Secretary of War canvassed the
merits of the various officers of the army, and
decided to place General Meade in command. Of
this decision General Meade was informed by a
dispatch sent by a special messenger, who reached
his quarters before the break of day the next
morning. It may be interesting to know the
grounds on which the President decided to promote General Meade.

First: That he was a good soldier, if not a
brilliant one.

Second: That he was a native of Pennsylvania,
and that State at that moment was the battle-field
of the Union.

Third: The President apprehended that a demand would be made for the restoration of General McClellan, and this he desired to prevent by
the selection of a man who represented the same
political opinions in the army and in the country.

Mr. Lincoln entertained advanced thoughts and
opinions upon all worthy topics of public con-
cern; indeed, his opinions were in advance, usually, of his acts as a public man. This is but
another mode of stating the truth, that he pos-

sessed the faculty of foreseeing the course of public opinion—a faculty essential to statesmen in
popular governments.

In 1853, in a campaign letter, he said : " I go
for all sharing the privileges of government who
assist in bearing its burdens. Consequently, I go
for admitting all whites to the right of suffrage
who pay taxes or bear arms, by no means exclud-
ing females." In 1854, he said : " Labor is prior
to and independent of capital. Capital is only
the fruit of labor, and could never have existed
if labor had not first existed. Labor is the support of capital, and deserves much the higher
consideration." In April of the same year, he
said : " I am naturally antislavery. If slavery is
not wrong, nothing is wrong. I can not remember when I did not so think and feel." In his
last public utterance he declared himself in favor
of extending the elective franchise to colored
men.

Thus he died, without one limitation in his
expressed opinions of the rights of men which
the historian or eulogist will desire to suppress
or to qualify. It is to be said further of this
many-sided man, and most opulent in natural
resources, that he takes rank with the first logi-
cians and orators of every age. His mastery over
Douglas in the debate of 1858 was complete.

While President, and by successive letters, he
effectually repelled the attacks and silenced the
criticisms of the New York Committee, of which
Erastus Corning was the head, that condemned
illegal arrests and the suspension of the writ of
habeas corpus; of the Union Committee of the
State of Illinois, that proposed to save the Union
if slavery could be saved with it; of the Democratic Convention of the State of Ohio, that denounced the arrest of Vallandingham; and of
Horace Greeley himself, when he complained of
the policy the President seemed to be pursuing
on the subject of emancipation.

As I approach my conclusion, I ask a judgment upon Mr. Lincoln, not as a competitor with
Mr. Douglas for a seat in the Senate of the United
States, but as a competitor for fame with the first
orators of this and other countries, of this and
other ages.

In support of this view I quote the closing
paragraph of his first speech in the canvass of
1858: "Our cause, then, must be intrusted to
and conducted by its own undoubted friends,
those whose hands are free, whose hearts are in
the work, who do care for the result. Two years
ago the Republicans of the nation mustered over
thirteen hundred thousand strong. We did this
under the single impulse of resistance to a com-

mon danger, with every external circumstance
against us. Of strange, discordant, and even hostile elements, we gathered from the four winds,
and formed and fought the battle through, under
the constant, hot fire of a disciplined, proud, and
pampered enemy. Did we brave all then to fal-
ter now? Now, when that same enemy is waver-
ing, dissevered, and belligerent? The result is
not doubtful. We shall not fail; if we stand firm
we shall *not fail.* Wise counsels may accelerate
or mistakes delay it, but sooner or later the victory is sure to come." We all remember his
simple, earnest, persuasive appeals to the South,
in his first inaugural address. At the end he
says: "I am loath to close. We are not enemies,
but friends. We must not be enemies. Though
passion may have strained, it must not break our
bonds of affection. The mystic cords of memory,
stretching from every battle-field and patriot grave
to every living heart and hearthstone all over this
broad land, will yet swell the chorus of the Union
when again touched, as surely they will be, by
the better angels of our nature." There is nothing elsewhere in our literature of plaintive en-
treaty to be compared with this. It combines the
eloquence of the orator with the imagery and
inspiration of the poet. But the three great papers on which Lincoln's fame will be carried

along the ages are the proclamation of emancipation, his oration at Gettysburg, and his second inaugural address. The oration ranks with the noblest productions of antiquity, and rivals the finest passages of Grattan, Burke, or Webster. This is not the opinion of Americans only, but of the cultivated in other countries, whose judgment anticipates the judgment of posterity.

When we consider the place, the occasion, the man, and, more than all, when we consider the oration itself, can we doubt that it ranks with the first of American classics? That literature is immortal which commands a permanent place in the schools of a country, and is there any composition more certain of that destiny than Lincoln's oration at Gettysburg? "Fourscore and seven years ago, our fathers brought forth upon this continent a new nation, conceived in liberty and dedicated to the proposition that all men are created equal. Now, we are engaged in a great civil war, testing whether that nation, or any nation so conceived and so dedicated, can long endure. We are met on a great battle-field of that war. We are met to dedicate a portion of it as the final resting-place of those who have given their lives that that nation might live. It is altogether fitting and proper that we should do this. But in a larger sense we can not dedi-

9

cate, we can not consecrate, we can not hallow
this ground. The brave men, living and dead,
who struggled here, have consecrated it far above
our power to add or detract. The world will
little note nor long remember what we say here,
but it can never forget what they did here. It
is for us, the living, rather to be dedicated here
to the unfinished work that they have thus far so
nobly carried on. . It is rather for us to be here
dedicated to the great task remaining before us;
that from these honored dead we take increased
devotion to the cause for which they here gave
the last full measure of devotion; that we here
highly resolve that these dead shall not have died
in vain; that the nation shall, under God, have a
new birth of freedom, and that government of the
people, by the people, for the people, shall not
perish from the earth." But if all that Lincoln
said and was should fail to carry his name and
character to future ages, the emancipation of four
million human beings by his single official act is
a passport to all of immortality that earth can
give. There is no other individual act performed
by any person on this continent that can be compared with it. The Declaration of Independence,
the Constitution, were each the work of bodies
of men. The Proclamation of Emancipation in
this respect stands alone. The responsibility was

wholly upon Lincoln; the glory is chiefly his.
No one can now say whether the Declaration of
Independence, or the Constitution of the United
States, or the Proclamation of Emancipation was
the highest, best gift to the country and to mankind. With the curse of slavery in America there
was no hope for republican institutions in other
countries. In the presence of slavery the Declaration of Independence had lost its power; practically, it had become a lie. In the presence of
slavery we were to the rest of mankind and to
ourselves a nation of hypocrites. The gift of freedom to four million negroes was not more valuable to them than to us; and not more valuable
to us than to the friends of liberty in other parts
of the world.

In these days, when politicians and parties are
odious to many thoughtful and earnest-minded
persons, it may not be amiss to look at Mr. Lincoln as a politician and partisan. These he was,
first of all and always. He had political convic-
tions that were ineradicable, and they were wholly
partisan. As the rebellion became formidable, the
Republican party became the party of the Union;
and, as the party of the Union, with Mr. Lincoln
at its head, it was from first to last the only
political organization in the country that consistently, persistently, and without qualification of

purpose, met, and in the end successfully met, every demand of the enemies of the Government, whether proffered in diplomatic notes or on the field of battle. He struggled first for the Union, and then for the overthrow of slavery as the only formidable enemy of the Union. These were his tests of political fellowship, and he carefully excluded from place every man who could not bear them. He accepted the great and most manifest lesson of free governments, that every wise and vigorous administration represents the majority party, and that the best days of every free country are those days when a party takes and wields power by a popular verdict, and guards itself at every step against the assaults of a scrutinizing and vigorous opposition. He accepted the essential truths that a free government is a political organization, and that the political opinions of those intrusted with its administration, as to what the Government should be and do, are of more consequence to the country than even their knowledge of orthography and etymology. As a consequence, he accepted the proposition that every place of executive discretion or of eminent administrative power should be occupied by the friends of the Government. This, not because the spoils belong to the victors, but for the elevated and sufficient reason that the chief offices of state are instrumentalities and agencies by which the majority carry out their principles, perfect their measures, and render their policy acceptable to the country; and also for the further reason that in case of failure the administration is without excuse. The entire public policy of Mr. Lincoln was the natural outgrowth of his political principles as a Republican. Through the influence of experience and the exercise of power the politician ripened into the statesman, but the ideas, principles, and purposes of the statesman were the ideas, principles, and purposes of the partisan politician. In prosecuting the war for the Union, in the steps taken for the emancipation of the slaves, Mr. Lincoln appeared to follow rather than to lead the Republican party. But his own views were more advanced usually than those of his party, and he waited patiently and confidently for the healthy movements of public sentiment which he well knew were in the right direction. No man was ever more firmly or consistently the representative of a party than was Mr. Lincoln, and his acknowledged greatness is due, first, to the wisdom and justice of the principles and measures of the political party that he represented; and, secondly, to his fidelity in every hour of his administration, and in every crisis of public affairs, to the principles, ideas,

and measures of the party with which he was
identified.

Having seen Mr. Lincoln as frontiersman, politician, lawyer, stump-speaker, orator, statesman,
and patriot, it only remains for us to contemplate
him as an historical personage. First of all, it is
to be said that Mr. Lincoln is next in fame to
Washington, and it is by no means certain that
history will not assign to Lincoln an equal place,
and this without any qualification of the claims or .
disparagement in any way of the virtues of the
Father of his country. The measure of Washington's fame is full; but for many centuries, and
over vast spaces of the globe, and among all peoples passing from barbarism or semi-servitude to
civilization and freedom, Mr. Lincoln will be hailed
as the Liberator. In all governments struggling
for existence, his example will be a guide and a
help. Neither the gift of prophecy nor the quality of imagination is needed to forecast the steady
growth of Lincoln's fame. At the close of the
twentieth century the United States will contain
one hundred and fifty or two hundred million
inhabitants, and from one fourth to one third of
the population of the globe will then use the English language. To all these and to all their de-
scendants Mr. Lincoln will be one of the three
great characters of American history, while to the

unnumbered millions of the negro race in the United States, in Africa, in South America, and in the islands of the sea, he will be the great figure of all ages and of every nation. His fame will increase and spread with the knowledge of republican institutions, with the expansion and power of the English-speaking race, and with the deeper respect which civilization will create for whatever is attractive in personal character, wise in the administration of public affairs, just in policy, or liberal and comprehensive in the exercise of constitutional and extra-constitutional powers.

It was but an inadequate recognition of the character and services of Mr. Lincoln that was made by the patriots of Rome when they chose a fragment from the wall of Servius Tullius and sent it to the President with this inscription: " To Abraham Lincoln, President for the second time of the American Republic, citizens of Rome present this stone, from the wall of Servius Tullius, by which the memory of each of those brave asserters of Liberty may be associated. Anno 1865." The final and nobler tribute to Mr. Lincoln is yet to be rendered, not by a single city nor by the patriots of a single country. A knowledge of his life and character is to be carried by civilization into every nation and to every people. Under him, and largely through his acts and influence, justice became the vital force of the republic. The war established our power. The policy of Mr. Lincoln and those who acted with him secured the reign of justice ultimately in our domestic affairs. Possessing power and exhibiting justice, the nation should pursue a policy of peace.

Power, Justice, and Peace; in them is the glory of the regenerated republic.

PRESIDENT LINCOLN.*

THE nation is bowed down to-day under the weight of a solemn and appalling sorrow, such as never before rested upon a great people. It is not the presence of death merely; with that we have become familiar. It is not the loss of a leader only that we mourn, nor of a statesman who had exhibited wisdom in great trials, in vast enterprises of war, and in delicate negotiations for the preservation of peace with foreign countries; but of a twice-chosen and twice-ordained ruler, in whom these great qualities were found, and to which were added the personal courage of the soldier and the moral heroism of the Christian.

Judged by this generation in other lands, and by other generations in future times, Abraham Lincoln will be esteemed as the wisest of rulers and the most fortunate of men. To him and to his fame the manner of his death is nothing; to the country and to the whole civilized family of man, it

---

* Eulogy delivered before the city government of Lowell, Massachusetts, April 19, 1865.

is the most appalling of tragical events. The rising sun of the day following that night of unexampled crime, revealed to us the nation's loss; but, stunned by the shock, the people were unable to comprehend the magnitude of the calamity. As the last rays of the setting sun glided into the calm twilight of evening, the continent was stilled into silence by its horror of the crime, and its sense of the greatness of the loss sustained.

To the human eye, Abraham Lincoln seems to have been specially designated by Divine Providence for the performance of a great work. His origin was humble, his means of education stinted. He was without wealth, and he did not enjoy the support of influential friends. Much the larger part of his life was spent in private pursuits, and he never exhibited even the common human desire for public employment, leadership, and fame. His ambition concerning the great office that he held was fully satisfied; and the triumph of his moderate and reasonable expectations was not even marred by the untimely and bloody hand of the assassin. During the canvass of 1864, and with the modesty of a child, he said: " I can not say that I wish to perform the duties of President for four years more; but I should be gratified by the approval of the people of what I have done." This he received; and, however precious it may have been to him, it is a more precious memory to the people themselves.

His public life was embraced in the period of about six years. This statement does not include his brief service in the Legislature of the State of Illinois, nor his service as a subordinate officer in one of the frontier Indian wars, nor his single term of service in the House of Representatives of the United States nearly twenty years ago. In none of those places did he attract the attention of the country, nor did the experience acquired fit him specially for the great duties to which he was called finally. He was nearly fifty years of age when he entered upon the contest, henceforth historical, for a seat in the Senate from the State of Illinois. This was the commencement of his public life, and from that time forward he gained and grew in the estimation of his countrymen. At the moment of his death, he enjoyed the confidence of all loyal men, including those even who did not openly give him their support; and there were many who came at last to regard him as a divinely appointed leader of the people. The speeches which he delivered in that contest are faithful exponents of his character, his principles, and his capacity. His statements of opinion were clear and unequivocal; his reasoning was logical and harmonious; and his principles, as then expressed, were consonant with the declaration, subsequently made, that "each man has the right by nature to be the equal politically of any other man." He was then, as ever, chary of predictions concerning the future; but it was in his opening speech that he declared his conviction, which was in truth a prophecy, that this nation could not remain permanently half slave and half free.

In that long and arduous contest with one of the foremost men of the country, Mr. Lincoln made no remark which he was unable to defend, nor could he, by any force of argument, be driven from a position that he had taken. It was then that those who heard or read the debate observed the richness of his nature in mirth and wit which charmed his friends without wounding his opponents, and which he used with wonderful sagacity in illustrating his own arguments, or in weakening, or even at times in overthrowing, the arguments of his antagonist. And yet it can not be doubted that for many years, if not from his very youth, Mr. Lincoln was a melancholy man. He seemed to bear about with him the weight of coming cares, and to sit in gloom, as though his path of life was darkened by an unwelcome shadow. His fondness for story and love for mirth were the compensation which Nature gave.

In the midst of overburdening cares, these characteristics were a daily relief; and yet it is but just to say that he often used an appropriate story as a means of foiling a too inquisitive visitor, or of changing or ending a conversation which he did not desire to pursue.

During the first French Revolution, when the streets of Paris were stained with human blood, the inhabitants, women and men, flocked to places of amusement. To the mass of mankind, and especially to the inexperienced, this conduct appears frivolous, or as the exhibition of a criminal indifference to the miseries of individuals and the calamities of the public. But such are the horrors of war, the pressure of responsibility, that men often seek refuge and relief in amusements from which in ordinary times they would turn aside.

In Mr. Lincoln's speeches of 1858 there are passages which suggest to the mind the classic models of ancient days, although they may not in any proper sense rise to an equality with them. His style of writing was as simple as were his own habits and manners; and no person ever excelled him in clearness of expression. Hence he was understood and appreciated by all classes. The Proclamation of Emancipation, his address at the dedication of the cemetery at Gettysburg, and his touching letter to the widowed mother who had given five sons to the country, are memorable

as evidences of his intellectual and moral greatness.

His speeches of 1858 are marked for the precision with which he stated his own positions, and for
the firmness exhibited whenever his opponent en-
deavored to worry him from his chosen ground,
or, by artifice, or argument, or persuasion, to induce him to advance a step beyond.

His administration, as far as he himself was concerned, was inaugurated upon the doctrines and
principles of the great debate. He recognized the
obligation to return fugitives from slavery, and it
was no part of his purpose to interfere with slavery
in the States where it existed. It must remain for
the historian and biographer, who may have access
to private and personal sources of knowledge, to
inform the country and the world how far Mr. Lincoln, when he entered upon his duties as President,
comprehended the magnitude of the struggle in
which the nation was about to engage.

The circumstance that his first call for volun-
teers was for seventy-five thousand men only, is
not valuable as evidence one way or the other.
The number was quite equal to our supply of arms
and material of war, and altogether too large for
the experience of the men then at the head of
military affairs. The number was sufficient to
show his purpose, the purpose to which he adhered

through all the trials and vicissitudes of this eventful contest. His purpose was the suppression of the rebellion, both as a civil organization and as an armed military force, and the re-establishment of the authority of the United States over the territory of the Union. There yet remain, in the minds of men who were acquainted with Mr. Lincoln in the spring and summer of 1861, the recollection of expressions made by him which indicate that there were then vague thoughts in his mind that it might be his lot under Providence to bring the slaves of the country out of their bondage. But, however this may have been, he never deviated from his purpose to suppress the rebellion ; and he conscientiously applied the means at his command to the attainment of that end. Thus, step by step, he advanced, until in his own judgment, in the judgment of the country, and of the best portion of mankind in other civilized nations, the emancipation of the slaves was a necessary means for the successful prosecution of the war. Mr. Lincoln was not insensible to the justice of emancipation ; he saw its wisdom as a measure of public policy ; but he delayed the proclamation until he was fully convinced that it offered the only chance of averting a foreign war, suppressing the rebellion, and restoring the Union of the States.

'In the great struggle of 1862, Mr. Lincoln ex-

hibited a twofold character. He was personally
the enemy of slavery, and he ardently desired its
abolition ; but he also regarded his oath of office,
and steadily refused to recognize the existence of
any right to proclaim emancipation while other
means of saving the republic remained. He
sought the path of duty, and he walked fearlessly
in it. Until he was satisfied of the necessity of
emancipation, no earthly power could have led
him to issue the proclamation ; and, after its issue, no earthly power could have induced him
to retract or to qualify it. When an effort was
madé to persuade him to qualify the proclamation, he said, in reference to the blacks, " My
word is out to these people, and I can't take it
back ! "

It has been common, in representative governments, for men to be advanced to great positions
without any sufficient evidence existing of their
ability to perform the corresponding duties, and it
has often happened that the occupant has not been
elevated, while the office has been sadly de-
graded. It was observed by those who visited
Mr. Lincoln on the day following his nomination
at Chicago, in June, 1860, that he would prove, in
the event of his election, either a great success or
a great failure.

This prediction was based upon the single fact

that he was different from ordinary men, and it did not contain, as an element of the opinion, any knowledge of his peculiar characteristics. History will accept the first branch of the alternative opinion, and pronounce his administration a great success. To this success Mr. Lincoln most largely contributed, and this in spite of peculiarities which appeared to amount to defects in a great ruler in troublous times.

Never were words uttered which contained less truth than those which fell from the lips of the assassin—" *Sic semper tyrannis !* "—as he passed, in the presence of an excited and bewildered crowd, from the spot where he had committed the foulest of murders, to the stage of the theatre whence he made his escape.

Mr. Lincoln exercised power with positive reluctance and unfeigned distaste. He shrank from the exhibition of any authority that was oppressive, harsh, or even disagreeable, to a human being. He passed an entire night in anxious thought and prayerful deliberation before he could sanction the execution of Gordon, the slave-dealer, although he had been tried, found guilty, and sentenced to death. There is but little doubt, such was the kindness of Mr. Lincoln's nature, that he desired to close the war, and restore the Union, without exacting the forfeit of a single life as a punishment for the great crime of which the leaders in this rebellion are guilty.

Could this liberal policy have been carried out, it would have been the theme of perpetual eulogy, and its author would have received the acclamation of all races and classes of men.

Mr. Lincoln had not in his nature, or in the habits of his life, any element or feature of tyranny. He had no love of power for the sake of power. He preferred that every man should act as might seem to him best; and when, in the discharge of his duties, he was called to enforce penalties, or even to remove men from place, he suffered more usually than did the subjects of his authority. It is easy to understand that this peculiarity was sometimes an obstacle to the vigorous administration of affairs. But, on the other hand, it must have happened occasionally that these delays led to a better judgment in the end.

Mr. Lincoln was, in the best sense of the expression, an industrious man. Whatever he examined, he examined carefully and thoroughly. His patience was unlimited. He listened attentively to advice, though it is probable that he seldom asked it. For nearly fifty years before he entered upon the duties of President, he had relied upon himself ; and it is said that, in the practice of his profession, he never sought opinions or suggestions from his brethren, except as they were associated with him in particular causes. He had the acuteness of the lawyer and the fairness of the judge. The case must be intricate indeed which he did not easily analyze, so as to distinguish and estimate whatever was meritorious or otherwise in it. He saw also through the motives of men. He easily fathomed those around him, and acted in the end as though he understood their dispositions toward himself.

He appeared to possess an intuitive knowledge of the opinions and purposes of the people. His sense of justice was exact; and, if he ever failed to be guided by it, the departure was due to the kindness of his nature, which always prompted him to look with the compassion of a parent upon the unfortunate—the guilty as well as the innocent. He was cautious in forming opinions, and disinclined to disclose his purposes until the moment of action arrived. He examined every subject of importance with conscientious care; his conclusions were formed under a solemn sense of duty; and while that sense of duty remained, he was firm in resisting all counter-influences. In unimportant matters, not involving principles or the character of his public policy, he yielded readily to the wishes of those around him; and thus they who knew him or heard of him in these relations only, were misled as to his true character.

No magistrate or ruler ever labored more zealously to place his measures and policy upon the sure foundation of right; and no magistrate or ruler ever adhered to his measures and policy with more firmness as long as he felt sure of the foundation. His last public address is a memorable illustration of these traits of character.

The charmed cord by which he attached all to him who enjoyed his acquaintance, even in the slightest degree, was the absence of all pretension in manners, conversation, or personal appearance. This was not humility, either real or assumed; but it was due to an innate and ever-present consciousness of the equality of men. He accorded to every one who approached him, whatever his business or station in life, such hearing and attention as circumstances permitted. For himself he asked nothing of the nature of personal consideration. In the multiplicity of his cares, in his daily attention to cases touching the reputation and rights of humble and unknown men, in the patience with which he listened to the narratives of heartbroken women, whose husbands, or sons, or brothers, had fallen under arrest, or into disgrace in the military or naval service of the country, he was indeed the servant and the friend of all.

The inexorable rules of military discipline were sometimes disregarded by him; he sought to make an open way for justice through the forms and technicalities of courts-martial, bureaus, and departments; and it is not unlikely that the public service may have received detriment occasionally by the too free use of the power to pardon and to restore. But the nation could well afford the indulgence of his overkind nature in these particulars; for by this kindness of nature he drew the people to him, and thus opinions were harmonized, the republic was strengthened, and the power of its enemies sensibly diminished.

Mr. Lincoln never despaired of the republic. During the dark days of July, August, and September, 1862, he was not dismayed by the disasters which befell our arms. His confidence was not in our military strength alone; he looked to the Lord of hosts for the final delivery of the people.

Following this attempt to analyze Mr. Lincoln's intellectual and moral character, it remains to be said that neither this analysis, nor the statements with which it is connected, furnish any just idea of the man. He was more, he was greater, he was wiser, he was better, than the ideal man which we should be authorized to create from the qualities disclosed by the analysis. And so, possibly, there will ever remain an apparent dissimilitude between the appreciable individual qualities of the man and the man himself.

Mr. Lincoln was a wise man; but he had not the wisdom of the ancient philosophers, who declared it to be the knowledge of things both divine and human, together with the causes on which they depend; but he was rather an illustration of the proverb of Solomon, "The fear of the Lord is the instruction of wisdom."

Mr. Lincoln must ever be named among the great personages of history. He will be contrasted rather than compared with those with whom he is thus to be associated; and, when compared with any, he is most likely to be compared with the Father of his Country. If this be so, then his rank is already fixed and secure. In many particulars he differs from other great men. When his important public services began, he was more than fifty years of age; while Cromwell was only forty years old when called from retirement, and most eminent men in civil and military life have been distinguished at an earlier age. He had neither military fame nor military experience. He was taken from private life, and advanced to the Presidency, upon a pure question or declaration of public policy—the non-extension of slavery. He entered upon his great office in the presence of assassins and traitors; and, from that day to the day of his death, he dwelt in their presence and faithfully performed his duties. He conducted the affairs of the republic in the most perilous of times. In the short period of four years he called three million men into the military service of his country. During his administration a rebellion, in which eleven States and six million people were involved, was effectually overthrown. But the great act which secures to his name all the immortality which earth can bestow, is the Proclamation of Emancipation. The knowledge of that deed can never die. On this continent it will be associated with the Declaration of Independence, and with that alone. One made a nation independent; the other made a race free.

There are four million people in this country who now regard Abraham Lincoln as their deliverer from bondage, and whose posterity, through all the coming centuries, will render tribute of praise to his name and memory. But his fame in connection with the Proclamation of Emancipation will not be left to the care of those who have been the recipients of the boon of freedom. The white people of the South will yet rejoice in the knowledge of their own deliverance through this gift to the now-despised colored man. And, finally, the people of the United States, of the American Continent, together with the whole family of civilized

man, will join in honors to the memory of him who
freed a race and saved a nation.

What fame that is human merely can be more
secure? What glory that is of earth can be more
enduring? What deed for good can be more wide-
spread?

The influence of the great act of his life will
extend to every continent and to all races. It will
advance with civilization into Africa; it will shake
and finally overthrow slavery in the dominions of
Spain and in the Empire of Brazil; and at last, in
that it saved a republic, and perpetuated a free
representative government as an example and
model for mankind, it will undermine the monarchi-
cal, aristocratic, and despotic institutions of Europe
and Asia. What fame that is human merely can
be more secure? What glory that is of earth can
be more enduring? What deed for good can be
more wide-spread?

Yet this great act rested on a foundation on
which all may stand. In the place where he was,
he did that which, in his judgment, duty to his
country and to his God required. This is, indeed,
his highest praise, and the only eulogy that his life
demands.

That he had greater opportunities than other
men, was his responsibility and burden; that he
used his great opportunities for the preservation

of his country and the relief of the oppressed, is his own glory.

Had Mr. Lincoln been permitted to reach the age attained by Jefferson or Adams, his death would have produced a profound impression upon his countrymen.

Had he now, in the opening months of his second administration, fallen by accident or yielded to disease, the nation would have been bowed down in inexpressible grief. Every loyal heart would have been burdened with a weight of sorrow, and every loyal household would have felt as though a place had been made vacant at its own hearthstone.

That he has now fallen by the hand of an assassin is in itself a horror too appalling for contemplation. Had the deed been committed in ancient Greece or Rome, we could not now read the historian's record without a shudder and a tear. All those qualities in the illustrious victim which we cherish were spurs, ever goading the conspirators on to the consummation of their crime.

His love of country and of liberty, his devotion to duty, his firmness and persistency in the right, his kindness of heart, and his spirit of mercy, were all reasons or inducements influencing the purposes of the conspirators. Neither greatness nor goodness was a shield. Had he been greater and bet-

ter and wiser than he was, his fate would have
been the same.

In this hour of calamity, let not the thirst for
vengeance take possession of our souls. But justice should be done. The circle of conspirators is
already broken and entered by the officers of the
law, and mankind will finally be permitted to see
who were the authors and who the perpetrators of
this great crime. For the members of this circle,
whether it be small or large, and whomsoever it
may include, there should be neither compassion
nor mercy, but justice and only justice. Judged as
men judge, this crime is too great for pardon.
The criminals can find no protection or harbor in
any civilized country. Let the Government pursue
them with its full power until the last one disap-
pears from earth. Vex every sea, visit every isl-
and, traverse every continent ; let there be no abid-
ing-place for these criminals between the Arctic
seas and the Antarctic pole !

This, Justice demands, as she sits in judgment
upon this unparalleled crime.

One duty and one consolation remain. He who
destroyed slavery was himself by slavery destroyed. Whoever the assassin, and however numerous the conspirators, love of slavery was the
evil spirit which had entered into these men and
taken possession of them. Slavery is the source

and fountain of the crime, and all they who have given their support to slavery are in some degree responsible for the awful deed. Let, then, the nation purify itself from this the foulest of sins. And this is our duty.

In the providence of God, Mr. Lincoln was permitted to do more than any other man of this century for his country, for liberty, and for mankind. Mr. Lincoln is dead ; but the nation lives, and the providence of God ever continues. No single life was ever yet essential to the life of a nation. This is our consolation and ground for confidence in the future.

GENERAL GRANT.

THE representative, republican system of government in the United States is no longer an experiment. In the period of the existence of this government, now nearly a hundred years, its Constitution has been perfected, its methods of administration improved, its faculties enlarged, its powers tested, and the limits of its authority and jurisdiction ascertained and established either by a recognized public opinion, or by the force of accepted judicial decisions.

While there are with us differences of opinion upon measures of administration, there are no substantial differences of opinion as to the fundamental principles of the government under which we are living. In this respect we are distinguished favorably from every other great government, unless a parallel can be found in the Oriental world. In England, Russia, Germany, and France, there are bodies of men who would welcome the overthrow of the existing forms of government, and the advent of a new order of things.

No system that is of human origin can be established more firmly than is the republican system of
government in the United States. This result is
due in part to the wisdom of men, but it is due in
a larger degree, probably, to what we are accustomed to call the force of events. But as the
events of which we speak are dependent, either
presently or remotely, upon the acts of men, it follows that the policy and doings of rulers of states,
and the achievements of leaders of armies, whose
acts may have tended to create, to preserve, or to
destroy states, must always engage the attention
of mankind.

It is therefore my purpose to consider some of
the events in the career of General Grant which
have contributed to the final and favorable solution of the problems that vexed the founders of this
Government.

In the first century of our national life three
persons have been elected to the presidency who
are, and who will continue to be, the three great
figures in American history : The Founder of the
Republic ; the Liberator of the Republic ; the
Savior of the Republic—

WASHINGTON, LINCOLN, AND GRANT.

They were not rivals in deeds ; and if some re-
semblances in character may be found, it is yet

true that they touched one another at a few points only.

As a soldier, Washington was equal to the demand made upon him; and as a recognized leader in the organization of a government upon ideas and principles for which there was no precedent, his pre-eminence is established.

Lincoln's fame rests upon his pure patriotism, his unyielding courage, and his great act of emancipation which made the restoration of the Union possible upon the basis of the equality of men in the States, and the equality of States in the Union.

The world-wide fame of General Grant rests upon his military achievements. As a soldier he has no equal in our history; and as a commander of armies he must be numbered in the first ten of whom the annals of mankind have taken notice.

I speak of General Grant as his friend, and in the hope that ultimately the world may see him on the page of history as he appeared to those who were near him when he was among the living. But I am not to use the language of bereavement, nor indulge myself in the utterance of funereal phrases. The days of mourning are over with the great public, and henceforth mankind will contemplate General Grant as an historical character only.

" The glory dies not, and the grief is past."

The greatness of men is manifested in what they are, in what they do, and in their capacity for foreseeing what is to be.

This test is applied to all the living, either by the family, or the neighborhood, or the State, or the nation; and it is applied to all the dead whose names and deeds finds a place in history. From that test we are not to shrink in this discussion. Things not attempted, or attempted and not accomplished, do not necessarily, nor even naturally, furnish either a test or a measure of a man's capacities. We value a machine by the measure of its strength at its weakest point; but we value a man by the measure of his strength at the place where he is strongest. Of absolute human greatness we have had no example; nor has it been the fortune of any man to be pre-eminent in a variety of ways. Usually the pre-eminence achieved has been limited to a single line of effort or sphere of duty.

The greatness of men is not found in a repetition of what has been done or said in other ages or by other men. The demand is for some new thought; some advance in scientific knowledge; some progress in art; some new idea in government; some feat, or stratagem, or campaign in war for which no precedent could be found in the ages; or some word or deed or policy by which nations are created, regenerated, or saved. And from this test we are not to shrink in considering the career of General Grant.

Greatness is not so much an acquisition as an endowment. The schools can not go beyond the known. They teach what has been accomplished. The sphere of the truly great man is outside or beyond the known. In that sphere the rules of the schools must be disregarded, or their teachings must be extended.

The influence of a great man will outlast the civilization in which he acts, of which he is a part, and to whose power he contributes. It may even outlive all knowledge of his name, it may course through unseen channels when nationalities, once vigorous, when forms of government once stable and controlling, when religions once believed and adored, have passed away and disappeared absolutely from the knowledge of men. All this can not be said or predicated of any living man, nor can any person assume as much of any contemporary, living or dead. This test is not in the present; it can only be made in the far-distant future. Nor can this claim be urged for any mere soldier, whatever his deeds, or however wide-spread may be his fame. The achievements of war must be interwoven with the fortunes of mankind in times of peace, and they must so work in institutions and

through the ages as to increase the happiness, elevate the character, and advance the destiny of men
in nations, or promote the progress of the race
generally.

In this particular the fortunes of General
Washington and General Grant are identical in
kind although they do not correspond in degree.
Washington's career in war was followed by the
successful reorganization of the States of the Confederacy of 1778, into a more perfect Union, but
still a Union in which there were serious defects.

The basis of our system of government is
found in the institutions of England and in the institutions of the colonies. The independent judiciary; the single executive, responsible to the people through the legislative branch of the Government; the Legislature composed of two Houses, of
equal powers in matters of legislation; and the
equality of States as constituents of the nation,
were all recognized as institutional features whose
incorporation into the new Constitution was a necessity arising from our history, traditions, and experience.

The debates of the Convention of 1787, the arguments of " The Federalist," and the commentaries
of Story upon the Constitution, all show that the
field for invention was limited. Our fathers bor-
rowed freely from Great Britain; they accepted

11

the lessons derived from the experience of the colonies, and especially the lesson taught by the failure of the Confederation. And, finally, they made concessions, not always without misgivings, and especially were there misgivings in reference to the concessions relating to the institution of slavery.

In 1787 there was a general impression that a new form of government was indispensable, but there was a wide difference of opinion as to what that government should be. There was a senti-ment of nationality, but that sentiment was subor-dinated generally to the hereditary attachment of the masses to the respective colonies and States. Some of the leaders feared that the sovereignty and pow-ers of the States would be absorbed by the General Government, while others apprehended that the Union under the new Constitution would crumble and fall from its own inherent weakness. To Washington is the country most largely indebted for the spirit of conciliation and for the mutual confidence which led the people to ratify the work of the Convention.

When Washington came to the presidency, the questions of pressing and paramount importance were these: The maintenance of the public credit; the payment of the public debt; the preservation of peace, while we asserted and vindicated all our just rights as one of the family of nations; and, finally, the organization of States, discordant in opinion and sensitive to every movement affecting their independence and sovereignty, into a compact political Union, capable of furnishing adequate protection, to citizens and States, against domestic violence and foreign foes.

All this was the work of administration when the Constitution had been prepared by the Convention, when it had been ratified by the people, and when the skeleton framework of the Government had been brought together; and all this was accomplished during the presidency of General Washington.

The claim of Washington to the appellation of " Founder of the Republic" rests not alone nor chiefly upon his services as commander of the armies, nor upon his services as President of the Constitutional Convention, but rather upon his foreseeing, conservative, organizing qualities and faculties manifested most clearly when he became President of the United States.

When General Grant became President, seven only of the eleven States then recently in rebellion had been admitted to representation in Congress. Georgia, Texas, Mississippi, and Virginia, were still held in a territorial condition and subject to military rule. The preceding three years had been

marked by a bitter contest between the executive
and legislative branches of the Government. In
ordinary times such a contest would affect perni-
ciously the welfare of a people. From 1866 to
1869 it was impossible for either party to the contest to originate and execute successfully any
system of reconstruction. The larger body of the
white inhabitants of the South took sides with
the President; the majority of the voters of the
old free States sustained the policy of Congress.
Under these diverse influences the restoration of
the States of the South was postponed, divisions
of opinion were promoted, which soon ripened into
bitter hostilities, all business interests languished,
and the day of substantial prosperity for the war-
stricken region of our country seemed farther away
than when Lee surrendered at Appomattox.

These evil influences were not limited by the
boundaries of the States that had been in rebellion.
The public revenues were either not collected, or
they were squandered or plundered on the way to
the Treasury. The payments on the public debt
for the year 1868 did not exceed twenty-five million dollars, while the total liabilities of the nation,
liquidated and unliquidated, were not less than
three thousand million. The annual interest account exceeded one hundred and thirty million
dollars.

The public credit was so impaired that coin bonds, bearing interest at the rate of six per cent, were sold at eighty-three cents on the dollar; the doctrine of repudiation was taught openly; and intelligent communities accepted the notion that the issue of irredeemable paper money was a safe and wise public policy. The country was divided, not very unequally, upon the question of extending the right of suffrage to the negro population of the South. The 27th day of February, 1869, five days before the inauguration of General Grant, Congress submitted to the States the question of the ratification of the proposition that is now the fifteenth amendment to the Constitution of the United States. Its fate was uncertain. By the fourteenth amendment a State was tolerated in denying to portions of its adult male citizens the right of suffrage if it would therefor consent to a proportionate loss of its representation in Congress and in the electoral college. It was an expedient adopted during the transition period between slavery and freedom. It was an expedient, moreover, that would have been fruitful in controversies if it had not been abrogated by the ratification of the fifteenth amendment.

In addition to these domestic difficulties our relations with France were disturbed by the recollection that Napoleon had attempted to place Maximilian upon a throne in Mexico in defiance of the Monroe doctrine, and at a moment when we were incapable of decisive action; the abolition of slavery in the United States and the revolutionary condition of affairs in Cuba had impaired our friendly relations with Spain; while with Great Britain there were causes of alienation and bitterness which, at any moment, might have led to the suspension of diplomatic intercourse.

This is but an imperfect summary of the difficulties, foreign and domestic, which confronted General Grant on the day of his inauguration. Assuredly they were less formidable than those which Mr. Lincoln had been called to meet in 1861, but, with that exception, they were the most serious difficulties that had waited upon any Administration since 1789.

Foreseeing is the primary element of statesmanship. This power General Grant possessed. In his inaugural address he said: "The country having just emerged from a great rebellion, many questions will come before it for settlement in the next four years which preceding Administrations have never had to deal with." He specified the questions, and he implored the country to deal with them "without prejudice, hate, or sectional pride." Again he said:

"A great debt has been contracted in securing

to us and our posterity the Union. . . . To protect the national honor every dollar of government
indebtedness should be paid in gold, unless otherwise expressly stipulated in the contract. . . . Let
it be understood that no repudiator of one farthing
of our public debt will be trusted in public place,
and it will go far toward strengthening a credit
which ought to be the best in the world, and will
ultimately enable us to replace the debt with bonds
bearing less interest than we now pay." Thus
clearly did he forecast the financial policy of his
Administration, and to that policy his Administration adhered. At its close, one fifth part of the
public debt had been paid, the interest had been
reduced in a greater ratio, the public credit was so
established that bonds bearing interest at four per
cent were at par, and the clamor for repudiation
was hushed absolutely.

"In regard to foreign policy," he said, "I would
deal with nations as equitable law requires individuals to deal with each other."   And he then served
notice on ambassadors, kings, and emperors in these
words : "*If others depart from this rule in their deal-
ings with us, we may be compelled to follow their precedent.*"   There was no departure from the rule,
and at the close of his Administration every international question had been adjusted amicably.

Thus and then, and for the first time in the his-

tory of the republic, every foreign question affecting the interests or rights of the nation was transferred from the field of diplomacy and debate to
the realm of fixed law. Questions between nations
imply controversy, and controversies may and often
they do develop into alienation and war.

As neither General Grant nor the American
people put any responsibility upon the French nation for the invasion of Mexico, the downfall of
Napoleon quieted all feeling on that subject.

A rigid observance of our neutrality, during the
rebellion in Cuba, preserved and strengthened our
friendly relations with Spain, and enabled the Administration to protest, and with effect, against the
system of slavery in the Spanish colonies.

With England we had one open question, as old
as our Government, which had given rise to acri-
monious correspondence in many Administrations.
The Island of San Juan, on the Pacific, had been
subject to joint armed occupancy for nearly a quarter of a century. By the treaty with Great Britain
of the 8th of May, 1871, that question was referred
to the arbitration of the Emperor of Germany,
who sustained the claim of the United States.

By the same treaty the claims against Great
Britain growing out of the destruction of our
commerce during the civil war, by vessels alleged to have been fitted out or to have obtained

supplies in British ports, were referred to arbitration.

The value of the arbitration was not so much in the adequate award that was made by the arbitrators, as in the example and precedent furnished and already followed by other nations as a means of avoiding war; and especially in the case of the reference by Germany and Spain of the question of the jurisdiction of the Caroline Islands to the head of the Catholic Church. But I should be unjust to the living, and I should misinterpret the sentiments and opinions which General Grant entertained and often expressed, if I did not say that the Administration and the country were largely, most largely, indebted to Hamilton Fish for the successful completion of these great undertakings in diplomacy. But I should be equally unjust to General Grant if I were to omit the statement that the policy of these negotiations was in harmony with his opinions, or that from time to time he contributed by suggestion and counsel to the result reached finally. Under our system the President is the responsible head of the Government; and while he can not, in the nature of his duties, supervise the details of the business of the departments, he does give direction to the policy of the Government, and most especially in its foreign affairs.

As in those affairs nothing can be accomplished

without his authority and consent, so at the end he should receive the praise, as he must, in case of failure, bear the blame.

The treaty of 1871 provided for the settlement of all the pending questions between Great Britain and the United States ; and it was a circumstance of unusual distinction that the terms of settlement were at the moment acceptable to the authorities and people of both countries.

The treaty of peace of 1783 left open for debate and controversy three questions of signal importance—the northeastern boundary, the fisheries, and the navigation of the Mississippi River.

The treaty of 1794 gave rise to bitter party contests in the United States ; it interrupted our friendly relations with France ; and, finally, it brought us to the verge of war with our ancient ally.

The purchase of Louisiana in 1803 was denounced as an unconstitutional proceeding, and eminent statesmen were filled with alarm at the extension of a territory which, as they thought, was already too vast for one government.

The treaty of peace concluded at Ghent, in the month of December, 1814, left open the question on which the War of 1812 had been declared.

The Ashburton - Webster treaty of 1842, by which the controversy in regard to our northeastern boundary was ended, and the danger of war with Great Britain averted, gave rise to disagreeable criticisms in Congress, and to violent opposition in the State of Maine, whose claims to jurisdiction were limited at points on its frontier.

The treaty of 1846, by which an effort was made to fix our northern line from the lakes to the Pacific Ocean, left to the two countries the inheritance of the San Juan controversy.

The treaty of 1871 with Great Britain takes rank as the third in importance of all the treaties to which the United States has been a party. First of all, the treaty of 1778 with France, of friendship and alliance ; then the treaty of peace with Great Britain of 1783, by which our independence was acknowledged and the foundations of our future greatness were laid.

Nor in this statement do I forget the signal advantages which have resulted from the treaty of 1803, by which the vast though not well-defined Territory of Louisiana was added to the domain of the republic.

Its acquisition was followed by some evils. Those evils were temporary ; the advantages were permanent. But the treaty did not originate any rule, nor settle any question of international law ; it did not quiet any controversy ; it did not avert any present pressing danger. Nevertheless, within the limits fixed by circumstances, the Louisiana treaty must ever be regarded as one of the wisest measures of American diplomacy.

To the world at large, however, the treaty of 1871 may prove to be the most important of any.

Our grievance against Great Britain was as serious as any grievance possible that did not arise from the actual invasion of territory.

The allegation then was—and the judgment at Geneva sustained the allegation—that Great Britain had covertly given aid and comfort to the rebellion, and that by that aid our commerce had been driven from the ocean, our prestige impaired seriously, and the commercial supremacy of England re-established for an indefinite period of time. Ancient hostilities were renewed, traditional prejudices were revived, and the war spirit of the nation might have been aroused easily and speedily.

By some the suggestion was made that England should be required to withdraw her flag from this continent. From others came the suggestion that we should lie in wait, and at a favorable moment retaliate upon British commerce.

To neither of these suggestions did General Grant give ear or voice. Trained to the art of war, acquainted with its perils and its horrors, the recipient of all the renown that nations can bestow upon a successful military chieftain, he was more than all a man of peace.

From the commencement of his Administration he felt assured of an ultimate settlement upon a basis honorable to the United States and not discreditable to Great Britain.

And may I not turn aside for a moment to indulge in the reflection that, under Providence, this great example may tend to the peace of nations? All Europe is oppressed by taxes and debts, and for every acre of her arable ground there is an armed man. This policy, if continued, can end only in general repudiation and universal disaster.

It may not be possible to avoid war. The intrigues of rulers, the ambitions of successful politicians and soldiers, the passions of the multitude, may involve nations in war; but the treaty of 1871 furnishes some security for the peace of the world. Or, if so much can not be assumed, it furnishes ground for the hope that considerate rulers will imitate the example and accept for guidance the new rules of international law which are embodied in the Treaty of Washington.

I pass now to the consideration of a topic on which differences of opinion exist.

Five days before the inauguration of General Grant, Congress adopted a resolution by which the proposition now embodied in the fifteenth amendment to the Constitution was submitted to the States.

In his inaugural address General Grant said : " The question of suffrage is one which is likely to agitate the public so long as a portion of the citizens of the nation are excluded from its privileges in any State. It seems to me very desirable that this question should be settled now, and I entertain the hope and the desire that it may be by the ratification of the fifteenth article of amendment to the Constitution."

General Grant was then at the height of his power and influence in the country. The incoming of his Administration marked a new epoch in public affairs. His political supporters, however, were not agreed in advocacy of the measure, and his opponents generally were hostile to the ratification of the amendment. If the President had been indifferent to its success, the proposition would have been lost. On that subject, however, his judgment was fixed and his purpose clear. Nor in that case was his judgment affected by the opinions or wishes of others.

He did not originate the measure, but his responsibility for the ratification of the proposed amendment is greater than that of any other person, living or dead. His reason for the recommendation is a living reason, and not unworthy present consideration by the whole country : " *The question of suffrage is one which is likely to agitate the public so long as a portion of the citizens of the nation are excluded from its privileges in any State."*

This is at once a prediction and a warning. The voice of the oppressed will at some time be heard. The demand of justice will at some moment be answered. Slavery employed its vast, concentrated power, re-enforced by the authority of the Government, for more than half a century, in an effort to stifle opinions, to suppress freedom of thought, of debate, and of political action, and the end was an inglorious failure and a retribution of blood.

The fifteenth amendment embodies the fundamental idea of republican, American liberty. It is the constitutional security for the political equality of men in the States, and without such equality there can be no equality of States in the Union. The injustice of men may delay, but the final result is not doubtful, nor even distant.

In these latter days the South has justly and freely accorded to General Grant high praise for the conditions and terms of the surrender at Appomattox. The circumstances of that occasion gave great dignity to the act, but the act itself was but the natural expression of the innate character of General Grant. In the nature of things the

leaders of Southern opinion could not have understood the hero of Appomattox in the year 1869;
but if it had then been given to them to see him as
he was, and if they had accepted the constitutional
amendments as binding and everywhere operative,
all of constitutional power that he could have commanded would have been used in aid of their re-
habilitation as States, and for the speedy development of their resources.

General Grant was free from malice, and he
was kind and compassionate by nature. It is difficult to comprehend the qualities of a man who
could be moved by a narrative of individual suffering, and who yet could sleep while surrounded by
the horrors of the battles of the Wilderness.

The solution of the difficulty must be found in
the fact that he possessed a philosophical temper-
ament which enabled him to look upon the consequences of war as of the inevitable, and to feel
that his duties, as the organizer and director of
armies, required him to suppress not only all manifestations of sympathy, but also to suppress the feeling itself. And this of a man whose devotion to
his family, to his friends, to his country, was absolute.

It is an error to assume that General Grant enjoyed the exercise of power, but it is true that he
enjoyed the possession of power as the evidence of

the public confidence. And it is an error of the gravest sort to assume that he had an ambition for the possession of arbitrary power. When the Ku-klux bands were engaged in their work of outrage and murder in the South, he sent a message to me requesting me to call at the Executive Mansion. When I met him, he said he had sent for me to accompany him to the Capitol. On the way he informed me that he had promised Senators that he would send a message to Congress asking for additional legislation for the suppression of the Ku-klux organizations. "But the public mind," said he, " is already disturbed by the charge that I am exercising despotic powers in the South ; and therefore I am unwilling to ask for additional legislation." Upon arriving at the Capitol, he sent for Senators and members, to whom he made known his change of opinion. With great unanimity they combated his views, relying mainly upon the proposition that it would be easier to defend the needed legislation than to defend the President in the steps that he might be compelled to take in the absence of specific authority.

While the discussion went on, General Grant turned to the table and wrote a message to Congress in favor of the proposed legislation. In the mean time, the Secretary of State and two other members of the Cabinet had arrived. Upon con-

12

sultation, one word only in the message was changed. This circumstance shows his disinclination to seek power, and it illustrates his facility in the use of his faculties when surrounded by distracting influences.

· In the administration of a government it happens occasionally that a person in office, or a person named as a candidate for an office, suffers unjustly through erroneous or false representations concerning him.

In General Grant's first term, a few persons were removed from office in the Treasury Department under such circumstances. When a case was within his knowledge, he never abandoned the person until some reparation had been made. Possibly the recollection of the wrong he had himself suffered might have quickened his sensibilities in that respect.

And let no one count these incidents as trifles, for they reveal the manner of man that General Grant was.

For the pomp and show of military life he had no taste whatever. He shunned military displays and reviews while in Europe. When in active service, his dress was plain, and he seldom wore a sword. He scarcely recognized the cheers of the soldiers, and he never sought them. His knowledge of military literature must have been limited. In many conversations that I had with him he never spoke of any military operation that did not relate to our civil war, or to the war with Mexico. When the citizens of Boston were about to give a library to General Grant, Mr. Hooper sought to ascertain, quietly, what military books the General owned, that duplicates might be avoided. He found that his library was barren of military works.

His respectable but not distinguished standing in his class at West Point was due to his mathematical powers, and not to his habits of study, nor to his attainments in other departments. He read novels, indulged his taste for sketching and painting, of which two specimens have been preserved, and he scanned the newspapers in the hope that Congress had abolished the school, that he might abandon military life without dishonor.

He obeyed the order to proceed to Mexico upon the idea that he was bound in honor to serve eight years in the army. Otherwise, he would have tendered his resignation at the close of his term at West Point.

General Grant was not a soldier from taste; his education at West Point was accepted, rather than sought; and he was not stimulated by the history and literature of war.

His appointment to the Military Academy was an incident which had no relation to his wishes nor to the opinions of any one as to his fitness for a military career. General Hamer, the member of Congress, and Mr. Jesse Grant, the father, were estranged from each other. Upon the failure of General Hamer's first appointee, he named young Grant as a tender of reconciliation. Ignorant of the names and persons of Jesse Grant's children, he combined in the letter of appointment the names of two of the boys, and thus gave to General Grant the initials U. S., which he was compelled to carry through his course at the Academy, though always under protest. Finally, General Grant accepted with satisfaction, and as a tribute to his mother, the change which General Hamer had made. This change of name, though wholly accidental and against the wishes of General Grant, was made the occasion of serious attacks upon his character in the campaign of 1868.

In estimating General Grant's claims to be considered a statesman, it is to be said, first, that statesmanship does not consist in the ability to look with equal favor upon the contending parties in politics. General Grant was a party man. He was not intense in his feelings, and he was always moderate in the expression of his opinions. In early life, he was a Whig. He thought that the war with Mexico was an unjust undertaking, and he took a part in it under a sense of duty to the Government that

had given him his education. He voted for Mr.
Buchanan in 1856, but for personal rather than political reasons.

At the opening of the war, he saw the issue, and
he accepted it.

In a letter to Mr. Washburne, dated August,
1863, he said : " It became patent to my mind early
in the rebellion that the North and South could
never live at peace with each other except as one
nation, and that without slavery. As anxious as I
am to see peace established, I would not therefore
be willing to see any settlement until this question
is forever settled."

This was a view, not of the soldier, but of the
statesman, and yet, there were men in the North,
in August, 1863, who were called statesmen, who
did not see that slavery was the cause of the war,
and that a permanent peace could be secured
only by its destruction.

If statesmanship be limited to those who pursue
their objects in politics and government by indi-
rect methods, then General Grant had no claim to
be called a statesman. His methods were as direct
in peace as they were in war. When he spoke, the
hearer knew exactly what the speaker then thought.
And if the subject of conversation concerned the
hearer, he might assume, safely, that he would be
advised at once of any change of opinion or purpose.

When he thought it unwise to express his views
or to declare his opinions he had the power to remain silent. Reticence, however, was not the
habit of his life nor the dictate of his nature, but
a custom to which he fled when his views were not
matured, or when the expression of them might
affect unfavorably a public measure or the fortunes of an individual.

He avoided councils of war, but by informal
conferences he gathered the views and received
the suggestions of the officers about him. Consequently, the orders that he gave did not overrule
the publicly-expressed opinions of any of his associates.

He had neither obstinacy nor pride of opinion.
At a critical moment in our foreign affairs the
President had received the impression that a new
policy in an important particular would be wise, or
he was at least considering the measure, and he
brought it to the attention of the Cabinet. When
two members had expressed opinions adverse to
the suggestion, and given their reasons, the President introduced a new topic, and he never again
referred to the subject.

In a limited sense he carried military ideas into
civil affairs. When and where he conferred power
he reposed trust and placed responsibility.

Neither as General of the Army, nor as President of the United States, did he assume to himself credit for what had been done by others. Indeed, he often accorded to his subordinates a larger share of credit than they claimed. And there is no surer test than this of real greatness.

Those who reach results only by dull, continuous labor are like the men who gather wealth by slow and tedious processes. Every gain stands for so much toil—burdensome toil, never to be forgotten. The great things of life are the products of truly great men. The labor with them is slight; the recollection is not husbanded; and there is always present the consciousness that other equally important results might be attained easily. Such men are not misers of deeds; they are not jealous; they are not harassed by the fear of rivals. They concede much to others, and they demand for themselves only what is freely accorded.

If we pause here, and exclude from our thoughts the Administrations of Washington and Lincoln, will General Grant suffer as a civil magistrate by a comparison with any other President of the Republic?

As a man, who more humane, more modest, more considerate of the rights of the humble?

As a magistrate, who more just in small things as well as great, or more devoted to peace, or more advanced in his ideas of Indian policy, or more scrupulous in the assertion of every national right, or more vigorous in the maintenance of the public faith, or more jealous of the honor of the country?

And which of all the other Administrations has done as much to diminish the public burdens, to lift up and to sustain the public credit ; and which of them all has done as much to ameliorate the bar- barism of war, or by a conspicuous example to avert war itself?

And, except Washington and Lincoln, who of all the long line of Presidents, to so great an extent, possessed the confidence and commanded the re- spect of princes and peoples throughout the civil- ized world?

In one particular General Grant was more fort- unate in his experience than either General Wash- ington or Mr. Lincoln. He visited the principal countries of the world, and he saw and conversed with their rulers. In foreign lands he made ad- dresses to public bodies, and, although he was not an orator, and although he was destitute of art or rhetoric in speech, he never uttered a sentence that an enemy could criticise or that a friend would blush to repeat. Educated by his knowledge of other forms of government and by an acquaintance with rulers—greater, I imagine, than was ever en- joyed by any other person—he returned from his travels not less an American in habit, in sentiment, in devotion to the country, than when he left Galena in 1861.

In the literary-political use of the word, General Grant was not a statesman. He was not learned in international law; he was not acquainted with the diplomatic history of Europe, nor can it be claimed that he was conversant with the diplomatic history of his own country.

He could not have originated and he would not have accepted any process or scheme of indirection in the business of government. His claim to statesmanship rests where his military fame rests. His qualities were practical. He saw things as they were. There was no glamour before his eyes, and he estimated the results of passing events with a degree of accuracy that seemed prophetic. But, more than all, his sense of justice could not be warped. Therefore he exacted of others only what they were bound to yield, and he was ready to grant to others what was right without delay and without debate. His statesmanship had no other art or magic in it than what may be found in the neighborhood relations of an honest country-people.

In General Grant's military career there were great days—steps by which he ascended to the heights at once so conspicuous and dazzling.

And begone forever the absurd idea that he was the child of luck, the favorite of Fortune; and begone the notion that, when he came to places of power and trust, places of power and trust were free from responsibility, peril, or danger of ruin! For twelve years in war and in peace, and for a period of three years and more when there was neither war nor peace, he stood in elevated and responsible places, and always exhibiting unbounded patriotism with adequate ability in peace, and an absolute supremacy of generalship in war.

These are not the accidents of any man's life. They are the natural results of innate power.

If, then, General Grant's successful military career was not an accident, it may be possible to discover some of the qualities or faculties on which his success was based. First of all, his skill to plan a movement or a campaign, and his ability to execute his plan, were in harmony. The ability to plan with coolness and care, and the power to execute with energy, celerity, and continuing fortitude, are not often combined in the same person. In all these qualities General Grant was highly endowed. His mind was occupied during the winter of 1862 –'63 with the plan of the campaign which ended with the commencement of the siege of Vicksburg in May, 1863. Sherman's march to the sea was forecast in a letter to General Sherman dated the 4th day of April, 1864.

Next, his topographical faculty was only less than real genius. In a military sense, his campaigns were in an unknown country. The region south of the Ohio and Potomac was, in a large part, destitute of good roads. It was covered by forests miles in extent and traversed by ranges of mountains in some sections and by rivers and bayous in others. No just comparison can be instituted between military operations in Europe, where well-built roads are described in books and laid down on maps, and kindred operations in the bottom-lands of the Mississippi, or in the wildernesses and swamps of Virginia, or the mountain-regions of Tennessee and Alabama.

The results indicate that General Grant could estimate with a reasonable degree of accuracy the value of a given number of men for defensive or offensive war. Very rarely was it true that his force at any given point was inadequate, and not often was there an excess. At the close of a day, whether his forces had been hard pressed or were victorious, his judgment was accurate, usually, as to the condition of the opposing army. Added to these high qualities, and in addition to a power, quality, or faculty, which can not be described nor specified, he had faith in the justice of

the national cause and faith in its ultimate triumph.

His experience in Mexico had enlarged, and,
without exaggeration, we may say that it had perfected, his training at West Point. He served under General Taylor and then under General Scott.
In his own language, he was in as many battles in
Mexico as it was possible for any one man to be in.
On several occasions he distinguished himself by
his courage, and by manifestations of that tact for
which he became conspicuous in the war of the rebellion. He left Mexico with an exalted opinion of
the military abilities of Taylor and Scott, and that
opinion he retained to the end of his life. He has
left, however, one criticism upon the conduct of
the war in Mexico. General Scott moved his army
from Vera Cruz in four divisions, a day apart, and
upon the same line. This order General Grant
criticises ; but he also criticises all his own campaigns, and says, finally, that the campaign against
Vicksburg is the only one which in his opinion
could not have been improved. General Grant
made mistakes, but it may not be judicious for a
civilian who never saw a battle, or for an officer
who never won a battle, to marshal the mistakes of
a general who never lost a battle.

When the blood of the men of Middlesex and
Essex was shed in the streets of Baltimore, General

Grant was eight days less than thirty-nine years of age. President Lincoln had already issued his call for seventy-five thousand men. General Grant responded to that call, and by his neighbors and townsmen, although he was not a voter, he was chosen to preside at a public meeting. By the aid of a prompter, but with a stammering tongue, he was able to state the purpose for which the people had convened. That was his first great day. Not distinguished by anything that he said or did. Not distinguished by his tender of service to the country. Tens on tens of thousands were then tendering their services and crowding forward for duty. To him and to the country it was a great day in the circumstance that it made possible his future career of usefulness and glory. In a military sense he was already a veteran. He had had fifteen years of training and service. But he made no demand for place; none for consideration on that account. No claim—no pretension. His neighbors and the authorities were left to form their own estimate of the value of his experience. But that day he gained a place to stand, and from it he moved the world.

He declined the captaincy of the company raised at Galena, but he went with it to Springfield, where he was employed first in instructing a clerk in the army methods of keeping accounts, and then in mustering and drilling the Illinois regiments for duty. Toward the end of May he made a tender of his services to the country through Lorenzo Thomas, then Adjutant - General of the Army of the United States. The letter was neither answered nor filed, and only recently was it rescued from the rubbish of the War Department! General Pope offered his aid, but General Grant declined, saying that he would not receive indorsements for the privilege of fighting for his country. Upon the second call for three hundred thousand men, Governor Yates commissioned Grant as colonel of the Twenty-first Illinois Regiment.

For the purposes of discipline the colonel marched his regiment from Springfield to Quincy. From thence it was moved to Mexico, Missouri, where Grant came to the command of three regiments. Just then, and upon an inspiration and without General Grant's knowledge, and in violation of the civil-service rules, the Illinois delegation in Congress recommended his promotion to the rank of brigadier-general.

His career had now commenced. He was assigned to a military district and to the command of an army larger than that of General Scott when he entered the city of Mexico—an army of brave men, but of men not yet disciplined to the hardships and duties of military life.

The battle of Belmont was fought the 7th day
of November. That was Grant's second great day.
Then his qualities as a commander were for the
first time tested. His army was composed of raw
recruits—brave men, stimulated to the verge of in-
subordination, by an anxious resolve to engage the
enemy. General Grant had two purposes in view :
First, to destroy the encampment at Belmont as a
means of preventing the re-enforcement of Sterling
Price, the Confederate commander in Missouri;
and, second, to discipline his troops by actual experience in war. The battle of Belmont was bravely
won ; but, when won, the discipline of the army was
lost, and only the genius of the commander saved
it from a disgraceful defeat that would have ended
in its dispersion or capture. General Grant was
the last man to leave the field, and he escaped capture by running his horse from the bank of the
river to the boat across a single gangway-plank.

Grant's winter-quarters were in Cairo, at the
junction of the Ohio and the Mississippi Rivers.
The Confederate troops still occupied Columbus,
Kentucky, a few miles below Cairo. There were
expeditions during the winter, and in the month of
January General Grant reached the conclusion that
the true line of operations was up the Tennessee
and Cumberland Rivers, on which were situated
Forts Henry and Donelson. That he might ob-

tain the sanction and authority of General Halleck, then in command of the department, he went to St. Louis and attempted to lay his plan before him. Without waiting for a full statement, General Halleck cut short the conversation, as if the plan were preposterous. Before the end of the month, however, General Grant obtained the co-operation of Admiral Foote, and then Halleck yielded to their joint request. In less than twenty days thereafter Forts Henry and Donelson had fallen under the combined operations of the army and the navy. By the surrender of Donelson about fifteen thousand men became prisoners of war, and all the material of the fort fell into our hands. The Confederate loss by capture, death, and desertion, could not have been less than twenty thousand men.

That was Grant's third great day. Great in the development of the character of the man, and great in the position attained. His letter to General Buckner, in answer to the proposition for an armistice, reads like the letter of Cromwell to the parsons of Edinburgh, and it is the most remarkable production to be found in military literature since the three memorable words of Julius Cæsar:

HEADQUARTERS, ARMY IN THE FIELD,
CAMP NEAR FORT DONELSON,
February 16, 1862.

General S. B. BUCKNER, *Confederate Army:*

SIR: Yours of this date, proposing armistice and appointment of commissioners to settle terms of capitulation, is just received. No terms except an immediate and unconditional surrender can be accepted. I propose to move immediately upon your works.

I am, sir, very respectfully,

Your obedient servant,

U. S. GRANT, *Brigadier-General.*

That day General Grant passed out from the ranks of the merely trained soldiers, and by universal acclaim he was admitted into the small body of tested, trusted, and successful commanders.

From that day forth he was to the nation the military chieftain on whom implicit reliance could be placed. And from that day forth the troops under his immediate command never apprehended a disastrous defeat, whatever might be the hardships and struggles and losses of a day or of a campaign.

Then for the first time the magnitude of things already accomplished revealed to General Grant the possibilities of the future—a future, filled with

13

greater events even, then opened, though indistinctly, before him.

Of all his countrymen, one only, as far as we have knowledge, and he his superior officer, hesitated to award due honor for what had been done, and he, upon the poor pretext that General Grant had neglected to report the force and condition of his command, suspended him from duty.

The 4th day of March, 1862, General Halleck suspended General Grant; and on the 13th day of the same month of March, with something of explanation and something of apology, he restored him to his command. Those nine days were sad, dreary days, when tears stood in the eyes of the discarded chieftain, but from his lips there was not one word of complaint.

The battle of Shiloh began Sunday, the 6th of April, and, although at the close of that day of blood our troops were still upon the field, our lines had been forced back toward the river, and a mile of ground had been lost. General Grant was lame and on crutches, from an injury caused by the fall of his horse; but he passed the night under a tree, exposed to a drenching rain, because he could not bear the sight of the wounded and dying men who were sheltered under a roof near by.

At the end of the next day a decisive victory had been achieved.

Important events followed.

General Halleck assumed the command of the army in the field. In a few weeks thereafter he was made general-in-chief. He then transferred his headquarters to the city of Washington, but it was not until the 25th of October that General Grant was assigned to the command of the department. Then for the first time was he in a position to devise and to act upon a comprehensive plan.

The rebel garrisons in Kentucky had then been abandoned. The Cumberland River was open to a point above Nashville, and the Tennessee was in our possession from its mouth to Eastport.

Much had been accomplished, but the Mississippi River was still held by the rebels at Vicksburg and Port Hudson. After the battle and victory at Corinth, in October, the movement on Vicksburg began.

The winter was spent in unsuccessful attempts to overcome the impediments interposed by the streams and bayous on the east and on the west of the Mississippi River, but in that winter, filled with toil, and suffering, and sacrifices, the final and successful plan of operations was matured.

General Grant originated the plan, and he believed in the possibility of its successful execution. And never was a commander better supported by his subordinates; and never, perhaps, was there a body of men, the officers, the rank and file, more united or more resolute in the purpose to accomplish what had been undertaken.

The passage of the batteries on the Mississippi River at Vicksburg by the gunboats and transports, the march of the army on the west bank of the river, the bridging of bayous, the crossing of the Mississippi, the landing upon the river-bottom between Bruinsburg and Grand Gulf, when the forces of the enemy within a circuit of fifty miles numbered not less than sixty thousand men, the battle and capture of the Highlands of Port Gibson, the battles and victories of Raymond, of Jackson, of Champion's Hill, of Black River Bridge, the final investment of Vicksburg, and all between the 16th of April and the 19th day of May, constitute a dramatic chapter in military history for which no parallel can be found in the annals of modern warfare.

To be sure, Vicksburg had not fallen, but its capture was made certain. The Confederate forces had been divided. One army was within the fortifications of the town, and soon to be subject to a close siege on all sides. The other army was to the south of the Big Black River, where it was confronted by General Sherman at the head of an adequate force.

In a few weeks, at farthest, Vicksburg and the army of Pemberton must surrender; the Mississippi River be opened for military purposes; the Confederacy divided, the supplies for the armies of the East diminished materially, and the downfall of the Confederacy itself made certain beyond the possibilities of chance or fate.

The surrender of Vicksburg, the 4th day of July, 1863, brought that memorable campaign to a close; and with its close and the victory at Gettysburg all thought of failure was banished from the minds of the loyal citizens of the North.

From this we turn now to his next great day.

The fatal battle of Chickamauga was fought on the 19th and 20th days of September, 1863. Rosecrans retreated with his disorganized army to Chattanooga, soon to be followed by General George H. Thomas, who had held his ground at Chickamauga. The Confederates established themselves on Lookout Mountain, at the southwest and west of the town, and also upon Missionary Ridge, which commanded the valley from the east and northeast.

General Bragg, then in command of the Confederate forces, constructed immediately a line of earthworks from the northerly point on Lookout Mountain to a point on Missionary Ridge near its southwestern extremity, and thence along the

Ridge to the north end. To the west was the long line of the Tennessee River, disappearing at the base of Lookout Mountain.

To the north was the only open passage through which supplies were received from Nashville over a devastated country and by a circuitous route not less than sixty miles in length. By the 20th of October the army was on half-rations, the animals were exhausted, and many thousands had died of starvation. A retreat under such circumstances would have resulted in the loss of the army. At that moment the Department of the Mississippi was created, which included all the ter-• ritory west of the Alleghanies, except the department of General Banks in the southwest, and General Grant was placed in command. General Rosecrans was relieved immediately, and General George H. Thomas was assigned to his place.

General Grant reached Chattanooga on the 23d day of October, at nightfall. At that time the Confederate authorities, civil and military, had no doubt about the surrender of our army in a few days, and upon such terms as they should dictate. This was the opinion of Jefferson Davis, who had visited the theatre of war the 15th day of October. On the 24th of October, the day after Grant's arrival, the orders of detail were issued for raising the siege of Chattanooga ; and, on the 27th, the orders had been so far executed that the Army of the Cumberland was free to receive supplies and re-enforcements, and as early as the 29th of October it was on an independent footing, with an abundance of supplies and material of war, and preparing for an offensive movement. That movement was made, and it terminated in the battle and victory of Missionary Ridge. General Grant's own words are not an exaggeration : " It would have been a victory to have got the army away from Chattanooga safely. It was manifold greater to defeat, and nearly destroy, the besieging army."

The fruits of the victory were six thousand prisoners, forty pieces of artillery, seven thousand stands of small-arms, and large quantities of other material of war.

The siege of Knoxville was raised and Burnside was set free, without a struggle, and without other assistance. Is it too much to claim that the Army of the Cumberland was saved by the presence and genius of General Grant? And, if not, then the day that he raised the siege of Chattanooga was a memorable day in his career.

He then came to the command of all the armies of the republic—numbering a million men—a greater force than ever elsewhere or at any other time recognized the rule and leadership of one man. Proportionately great was the field of operations. Its boundaries were the line of the Mississippi River, the frontier from beyond the Mississippi to the Atlantic Ocean, then along the coast of the Atlantic and the Gulf of Mexico to Texas, with one army penetrating to the center of the Confederacy and others moving upon and besieging Richmond ; and all without instructions from the President or War Department, and all without the aid of a council of war. The end was the surrender of Lee and the army of brave men who had stood at the gateway of the Confederacy for four years : Richmond fell, the leaders of the rebellion were dispersed, and the Union was saved.

That was the great day of General Grant's life, and of the results of that day's doings no power, that is human merely, can form a just estimate. He lived to see the Union he had so contributed to save compacted and in a good degree harmonized. Not only had the institution of slavery disappeared, but the ancient faith in the economy and rightfulness of slavery had disappeared also. Of all the millions of his fellow-citizens there was not one in power or station who ventured to avow his hostility to the Union, or to the fundamental institutions of the Government under which we are living. These are the fruits of a victory to be enjoyed by us and by our successors through many,

many generations—fruits to be shared equally by the vanquished and by the victors.

From that day forth the United States has been recognized as one of the leading nations of the world. Upon the opening of the rebellion in 1861, the enemies of republican institutions accepted the event with satisfaction, as furnishing proof conclusive that such institutions could not be maintained. The surrender of Lee in 1865 banished that idea from the minds of statesmen the world over.

The tendency now everywhere is to local self-government, the aggregation of small states, the concentration of powers for national and international purposes, coupled with a system of responsibility on the part of the Executive.

It was the theory of dynastic rulers that popular governments were limited to small states. That error has now passed away, but by all former generations of European statesmen the United States was not treated as an exception.

At present the attention of the world is fixed upon our system of government. Here institutions are free; here everywhere there is local self-government; here, generally, the equal political rights of men are acknowledged; here our institutions recognize no distinctions of race, and the thought of such distinctions is fast disappearing from the public mind; and here the central Government is endowed with ample powers for every exigency of national life. Here every man is a citizen, and every citizen is at the same time a member of the ruling class and a member of the subject class. The germs of this policy of national life, minute in its details and comprehensive in its scope, are found in the institutions of the colonies North and South, but their development was delayed until the Confederacy was overthrown, slavery destroyed, and the extreme doctrine of State rights had perished.

The new Government rests upon co-ordinate political propositions—the equality of men in the States and the equality of States in the Union. The old Constitution recognized the equality of States, but there was no national citizenship and no recognition of the equality of men.

Neither in principle nor in public policy was the change as important from the rule of George the Third to the Administration of General Washington, as from the Administration of James Buchanan to that of General Grant at the commencement of his second term.

In this later period old ideas disappeared ; old institutions crumbled and fell ; new ideas were developed, and new institutions were created.

The overthrow of the Confederacy made possible all these changes. The future of America was shaped by that event. The nation accepted the new ideas, it created new institutions, and it entered upon a new career.

It is not for this day nor for this generation to estimate General Grant's share in contributing to these events so accomplished.

The Proclamation of Emancipation was made practical, absolute, and irreversible by the victories of General Grant. The Proclamation of Emancipation made the victories of General Grant possible. Thus, by the combined labors of Lincoln and Grant, the system of slavery was abolished, and the Union re-established on the basis of the equality of men in the States and the equality of States in the Union. Thus are they united in fame, and thus are they destined to a common inheritance of glory.

History will reject the language of eulogy, but it must deal with the important events which signalize General Grant's military career. And can it fail to place him with the small number of great generals since Julius Cæsar?

The successes of life are not accidents. For four years General Grant was tested by the severest ordeals. Other men might have saved the country; but he only had the opportunity and the capacity to save the country. If, upon the record of General Grant, we deny to him intellectual power of a high order, as well as genius in affairs of war, we have then no longer a test of greatness or superiority among men.

Thus have I attempted to communicate my impressions concerning General Grant. I knew him when he was in health, in prosperity, and in power. I knew him when he was borne down by adversity and assailed by a fatal disease. In all conditions he was the same man. No change of fortune could change his character. He was imperturbable in spirit, obedient to the demands of justice, constant and faithful in his friendships, and to the last he was devoted to the country that he had served and saved.

GENERAL GRANT—THIRD TERM.*

In politics, morals, and law there is a field for presumption. The field is a limited one, usually, but within it the conclusions drawn are as trustworthy as are those which, in the broader field of testimony, rest upon positive proof.

In politics, and in the light of this day, no presumption can be more just and reasonable than the presumption that every Democrat is opposed to the election of General Grant to the presidency for a third time. And this opposition by Democrats is not on account of the example of Washington, or of the tradition of a century, or of the resolution of the House of Representatives of 1875; for they were quite as fiercely opposed to his first election in 1868, to his second election in 1872, when the example of Washington was inapplicable, when the tradition of the fathers could not be cited, when the resolution of the House of Representatives did not exist.

Among Democrats the most conspicuous Demo-

* From " The North American Review," April, 1880.

crat in this opposition to General Grant was Judge
Black, of Pennsylvania; and, in the March number
of "The North American Review," he gives his
friends the benefit of his argument against the
third election of General Grant, and inflicts upon
his enemies the full force of his passions. He has
seen nothing good or even hopeful in the events
of the last twenty years; and he has read of nothing bad in the annals of Rome, where chiefly his
studies appear to have been, whether as republic or
empire, which he does not apprehend for America
in case of the election of General Grant for a third
term. His argument against the election of any
person to the presidency a third time is based
upon the example of Washington and the declara-
tions of Jefferson. The authorities are good, and,
when there was no trustworthy history, either for
example or warning, except that of ancient Rome
and the histories of the mediæval and feudal states
of Europe, the argument itself was not bad.

In the course of his article Judge Black has
made many references to ancient Rome. His ex-
cellence herein is admitted. At best I can make
but one. Gibbon says of the various modes of
worship which prevailed in the Roman world that
"all were considered by the people as equally true,
by the philosophers as equally false, and by the
magistrates as equally useful." There is no vio-

lence in the assumption that Judge Black has been
so absorbed by the thought that the example of
Washington and the teachings of Jefferson could
be made *useful* to the Democratic party in this its
exigency, that he has neglected to consider with
care the question whether, after a century of experience in free popular government, it is indeed true
that the example of Washington in this respect is
the only remaining bulwark for the protection of
our assailed and imperiled liberties. If this be so,
then the reputation of Washington will need a
more ardent—perhaps I may not be permitted to
say a more able—defender than even Judge Black
himself.

Washington was President of the Convention
which framed the Constitution of the United
States. That Constitution makes every male citizen who has attained the age of thirty-five years
eligible and re-eligible, without limitation as to
times, to the office of President of the United
States. If the peril to the country from the repeated election of the same person to the presidency was believed by Washington and his associates to be such as Judge Black now represents it,
then Washington and his associates are wholly
without excuse in their neglect of a great public
duty. Nor is it an answer or defense to say that
Washington intended to leave an example to his

countrymen which, in the course of time, would, as a tradition, become as powerful for the protection of their rights and liberties as would be a written constitutional inhibition. Life is uncertain; death is certain; and in 1787 Washington could have had no assurance that he would be permitted by Divine Providence to hold the office of President for eight years, and at the close to give an example of voluntary abstention from worldly honors which should not only receive the approval of the living generation, but also command the respect and obedience of his countrymen in all ages of the republic.

Mr. Jefferson was not a member of the Convention, and it is well known that its proceedings in many particulars were not approved by him. But to Mr. Jefferson, more than to any one else, is the country indebted for the first eleven articles of amendment to the Constitution—articles designed to render the liberties of the people more secure against the encroachments of power. But these amendments are silent in regard to the presidential office. Provision is made, however, that persons charged with crime shall have a perpetual constitutional right to compulsory process for obtaining witnesses in their favor; that in all suits at common law, where the value in controversy exceeds twenty dollars, the right of trial by jury shall be preserved; and yet no constitutional safeguard is

erected against a manifest peril, a continuing menace to the institutions and liberties of an entire
people.

If Washington and Jefferson estimated the peril
as Judge Black now says the peril was estimated
by them, and as in fact the peril really is, who is
sufficient to offer a defense, an excuse, or even an
apology for the Father of his Country or the Apos-
tle of Liberty? The original Constitution was
wrought out in the presence and under the lead of
Washington, and the amendments were framed at
the dictation of Jefferson. Eight words in the
Constitution or in an amendment would have furnished ample protection for all time. The words
are not there, and why not? Surely not because
Washington and Jefferson were not patriotic men,
nor because they were not far-seeing men, but because upon reflection they thought it unwise to
place any limitation upon the power of the people
to elect their rulers at stated times and in pre-
scribed ways. The country is not lacking in veneration for Washington and Jefferson. That veneration will survive the criticism of Judge Howe,
it will outlive the defense of Judge Black. And
may one inquire whether there is anything in the
example of Washington which warrants the opinion that this Government has not constitutional
power to protect its own life; or anything in the

14

teachings of Jefferson inconsistent with the emancipation of the slaves, their elevation to citizenship,
their equality under the Constitution of the country; or if there is anything in the example or
teachings of Washington or Jefferson which justi-
fies Judge Black and the party that he represents
in the attempt that was made to overthrow the
Union, in the resistance to emancipation, and in the
continuing effort to subvert the Government by
the forcible suppression of the popular will? In
every age there are those who build the tombs of
the prophets and garnish the sepulchres of the
righteous, and yet deny justice to the living generation of men.

If Judge Black's argument against a third term
shall receive only that degree of favor which has
been accorded to his public teachings for the last
twenty years, he may be assured that the chief reason is to be found in the conduct of the party with
which he is identified. That conduct has awakened the most serious apprehensions in the public
mind touching the security of property and of personal political rights; and these apprehensions not
only justify but require the people to place the
helm of government in the hands of the man best
qualified to guide the ship of state safely through
stormy seas. In quiet times the tradition of the
fathers would be respected, and this without a

careful examination of its value or of its applica-
bility to modern affairs. It is to the teachings of
Judge Black, and the associates of Judge Black,
that the country is indebted for the circumstances
in our public life which compel us to canvass the
tradition upon its merits, to examine the circumstances in which it had its origin, and to consider
and determine whether its authority is such, or its
intrinsic value such, that in a grave exigency in
public affairs, and in obedience to that tradition
alone, the man best qualified to protect personal
rights and to defend public interests shall be excluded from the public service. If a strong man
is needed at the head of the Government, the necessity arises from the circumstance that the spirit
of rebellion, of resistance to the Constitution, is
manifested by a large class of citizens. Those citizens, without exception, are Democrats, and they
receive aid and encouragement from the Democratic party. It is the purpose of the Republican
party to suppress that spirit; to render it power-
less, absolutely, both in personal and in public
affairs. And it may happen that, in accomplishing
this result, the example of Washington and the
tradition of the fathers will be disregarded. I admit the example, I recognize the tradition, and,
with these admissions, it is my purpose to consider
their binding force upon the country, their histori-

cal origin, their intrinsic value as guides in public affairs.

There has been a serious effort to establish the proposition that what is called "the tradition of the fathers" is as binding upon the country as a limitation upon the power of the people would be if the restriction were a part of the Constitution itself. Judge Black sustains the notion, and gives to it the benefit of his rhetoric and his emphasis. Statement alone is sufficient upon this point. Argument is unnecessary. The opinions of Washington and Jefferson are entitled to the highest consideration as opinions—nothing more. We refuse to allow the hands of dead men to control the soil of the country; and shall we without inquiry, without a judgment of our own, permit the opinions of dead men to control the thought and the policy of the country? We have changed, indeed in some particulars we have annihilated, the Constitution of Washington, the Constitution of the fathers, and therefor take equal honor for ourselves and for them, in the belief that if they were among us they would accept and ratify with acclaim the changes that have been made.

And is the unwritten law more sacred? May the people annul the written law of the fathers, and still be bound perpetually by their traditions? It would not be strange if in these later days, and for a particular reason, the importance of Washington's example had been unduly magnified. When he prepared his Farewell Address to his countrymen, the most important document that ever came from his pen, he omitted all reference to his own example in retiring from the presidential office at the end of the second term, as imposing upon all his successors a corresponding practice. In November, 1806, the Legislature of Vermont nominated Mr. Jefferson for a third election to the presidency. If he had then realized the dangers of such a proceeding as they are now set forth by Judge Black, would he have waited till December, 1807, before he announced his purpose not to be a candidate for re-election?

It is a satisfaction that, even at this somewhat advanced stage of the discussion, I am in accord with Judge Black upon one point. He says, "The mere authority of names, however great, ought not to command our assent." This is a sound proposition in ethics, in politics, and in law. All through these weary pages I am endeavoring to demonstrate its wisdom in matters of politics, and I relieve the tediousness of the hour by a single illustration designed to show its importance in matters of law.

Judge Black, speaking of real estate, and not of politics, says, "A lease for years, renewable and always renewed, gives the tenant an estate without end, and makes him lord of the fee." This sentence is admirably turned, and its rhetoric is above criticism or complaint: but as a legal proposition it is only true when some words, possibly implied by the writer, are clearly expressed. It should be written, "A lease for years, renewable *at the will of the tenant*, and always renewed, gives the tenant an estate without end, and makes him lord of the fee"; and, thus written, its inapplicability to the question under discussion is fully exposed. The tenure of the office of President of the United States is not renewable at the will of the tenant, and therefore the tenant can never become lord of the fee. It is only renewable at the will of the lord of the fee—the people; and, being so renewable only, the fee must ever remain in the lord, however often the lease may be renewed.

But it is not open to doubt that there has been a general disinclination in the American public mind to the election of the same person to the presidency a third time; and there is as little doubt that that disinclination is less general and less vigorous than it was three years ago. It is, however, as old as the Government. It had its roots in the experience of the colonists. In Europe hereditary power had fostered standing armies, and standing armies had maintained hereditary power. Both were the enemies of personal liberty and popular rights. It was the purpose of the founders of our Government to render standing armies unnecessary, and the possession of heredi- tary power impossible. If the experience of a century is an adequate test, the end they sought has been attained. They had observed, also, that the possession of power, by virtue of office, for un- limited periods of time, tended to the establish- ment of dynastic systems and to their recognition by the people. Hence provision was made in all our Constitutions, State and national, for frequent elections in the legislative and executive depart- ments of Government. But these apprehensions, whether wise or not, did not lead the founders of the republic to the adoption of a system which limited the powers of the people or cast a doubt upon their capacity for self-government.

The term of the presidential office was limited to four years, but the constitutional ability of the people to continue one person in the office through many terms was admitted without limit. If the men who framed the Constitution apprehended evils from a third or even a second election of the same person to the presidency, they accepted those possible evils in preference to a limitation of the power of the people in the choice of their rulers. The tenure of office is fixed, but the Constitution is silent upon the question whether it is wise or unwise to continue the same person in office for more than one term.

Washington avoided a third term, and his example has had large influence in leading the country to accept the opinion that a contrary policy is fraught with danger to the public liberties. Washington's motives and reasons are not clear. He was, however, no longer young. His best years had been spent in the public service, and he naturally yearned for the peace and quiet of private life. Nor can there be a doubt that, superadded to these personal considerations, was the thought that his example might serve as a restraint in case of the appearance of a popular leader who should seek to subvert the Government through successive elections to the presidency.

The system of government which Washington and his associates had inaugurated was a novel system. Government of the people, by the people, and for the people was an experiment. No one could then foresay what their capacity would prove to be in emergencies, or even in quiet times. The power of rulers in dynastic countries was much more absolute a century ago than it now is, and the extent of that power measured the danger to which, in the estimation of our fathers, free peoples were exposed.

Washington's example was set off and made impressive by the phenomenon of a Corsican corporal passing at a bound, as it were, from the ruins of a republic to the throne of an empire, displacing kings and rulers, and founding a family dynasty that has lasted nearly a century, either in power or contending for power.

The experience of Europe gave rise to the opinion in America that it is dangerous to permit the same person to continue in the chief executive office for a long period of time; but the traditionary idea that the danger-line in the presidential office is the line between the second and third terms, is due to the influence of Washington's example.

Aside from governments in which office is conferred by popular suffrage constitutionally enjoyed and exercised, there are three methods of gaining and holding power:

1. Physical force. 2. The claim of a right to rule, sometimes called the divine right to rule, which is the result of the enjoyment of power in a family for a long period of time. 3. Recognized mental and moral supremacy.

As to the first mode—the establishment of a personal or family government in the United States by physical force—it is to be said that the success of such an undertaking, or even its attempt, is too remote in the logic of events, and too improbable when judged by experience or tested by reason, to warrant argument or to command attention. The destruction of a government is always a possible fact, and no one can predict the consequences; but, if its overthrow is by force, the aggressive actors are parties out of power, and its defense, whether vigorous or weak, is by those in power.

Moreover, it is to be said that the opportunity for a president to seize the Government by force is as great in the first or second term as it can be in the third; and the probability that a man who had not been tempted, or who had not yielded, in the first and second terms would prove faithless in the third, is a view of human nature contrary to all human experience. And there is less probability that the possession of the presidency for eight, or twelve, or twenty years would induce even one person in the United States to admit a divine right to rule either in the occupant of the office or his family.

Lastly, if mental or moral supremacy were recognized, that recognition would find expression in the United States by an election through constitutional means.

There are two theories of political action, theories inconsistent with each other, both unsound and both maintained and propagated by the same body of theorists in matters of government. One theory is that men in subordinate places should be continued in those places as long as they are faithful and competent, and this without regard to their political opinions or to the qualifications of contestants; and the other theory is that in the chief place of government, where experience, capacity, and integrity are of more consequence than in any subordinate place, the occupant should be excluded after four or certainly after eight years' experience, however competent, wise, and just he may have proved himself to be. If a public policy were to be based upon reason, the stronger arguments would be found in favor of continuing the President in office as long as his services were acceptable to the people.

In truth, however, there is no field for argument. No man has a right to an office, but it is the right of the people to select men for place who in their opinion are best qualified to do the work they wish to have done.

Where, by the Constitution, appointments are vested in the President, in the courts, or in the heads of departments, the same right rests in those constitutional agents of the people ; and it becomes their duty to continue men in office when the public interests will be best promoted by so doing, and to remove men from office when their places can bc supplied by persons more capable of rendering efficient service. There can be no title to office, and there ought to be no rule of absolute exclusion from office.

In public affairs, as in private life, it is true usually that our apprehensions are not awakened by the dangers that actually menace us. Executive power and the influence of office-holders are the dangers apprehended that now most excite the public mind. It may not be out of place to say that there are less than eighty thousand office-holders under the national Government, and that of these not twenty thousand are appointed by the President directly, the rest receiving their commissions from heads of department and the courts. This army of office-holders numbers one to about six hundred inhabitants, and there are probably not another eighty thousand intelligent men in the country whose political influence is less than theirs. If they support an Administration, they are characterized as sycophants; if they put themselves in opposition to it, they are branded as ingrates; and if they are silent, they are treated as cowards. There is indeed no place in politics for an office-holder by. executive appointment where he can exert the influence that is accorded to an independent, energetic private citizen. Office-holders should be free to express their opinions ; above all, they should be free from any constraint proceeding from the appointing power ; but in no aspect of affairs are they a dangerous class in our politics. And it is a kindred weakness to suppose that the liberties of the country are in danger from executive powers. Executive authority is diminishing in China, Japan, Russia, Germany, and England, and in all those countries the jurisdiction of the legislative branches of government is broader, firmer, and more respected than ever before. With us power tends toward Congress, and in Congress to the House of Representatives. In these four years we have seen the just and proper authority of the President restrained and paralyzed by the House of Representatives, and during the Administration of Andrew Johnson his dispositions and purposes were checked and thwarted by the same branch of the Government.

The liberties of the country can not be subverted as long as that branch of the Government which can open and close the Treasury of the nation at its sovereign will is true to its duty ; and that branch will remain true to its duty while the constituency is both intelligent and honest. I venture to assert that there is no present danger from the comparatively small body of office-holders, none from presidential patronage, and nothing of imminent peril, indeed, from the numerous evils marshaled under the term *maladministration,* from which no country is ever entirely free.

With these observations upon questions of minor importance, I turn to the one topic of supreme interest and of real peril—the purpose of the old slaveholding class to subvert the Government by securing the rule of a minority, first in the South, and then consequently in all the affairs of the republic ; and I shall then proceed to show how this purpose may be most successfully thwarted by the election of General Grant.

We all know that this undertaking in the end must prove a failure ; but the speedy overthrow of the scheme, and the speedy dissipation of the idea on which the scheme rests, are essential to the reputation and welfare of the country. On the other hand, the prosecution of the scheme is an obstacle to business, a constant peril to the public peace, a direct assault upon the interests of labor in every section, and a menace to free government in all parts of the world. It is a delusion, a criminal delusion, to accept the notion that there can be unbroken peace and continuing prosperity while any number of citizens are, as a public policy of communities and States, deprived of their equal rights.

And it is a delusion not less criminal and even more dangerous to accept the suggestion that the old free States, containing a majority of the people of the country, will peacefully, and through a series of years, submit to the rule of men in the executive and legislative branches of the Govern-ment, who take office and wield power through proceedings that are systematically tainted with fraud or crimsoned with innocent blood.

It is clearly established beyond the demands of legal or moral proof that there are persons in the Senate of the United States who have no better right in equity to the places they occupy than they have to seats in the Commons of Great Britain. The same is true of the House of Representatives, and these persons constitute the majority in each branch. Thus has our former indifference to the fortunes of our brethren in the South been visited by a direct penalty upon ourselves.

I proceed now to state our demand of the South, and in that statement I disclose also the evil of which we complain.

Our demand, speaking generally, is, that in all the States of the Union every person who has a right to vote shall be permitted to vote ; that his vote shall be counted ; that it shall be honestly val-ued ; and that the governments created by the ma-jorities shall be set up and recognized. The con-test is upon this proposition, and upon this propo-sition the contest will be waged until it is accepted, practically, in all parts of the Union. Not from

hostility to the South will this contest be carried
on ; but in regard to the rights of our fellow-citizens there and in defense of our rights as citizens
of the republic will the contest be prosecuted to
the end, whether near or remote. Under the system of suppression and wrong now existing, the
vote of a white citizen in South Carolina or Mississippi is, as a fact in government, equal to the
votes of three citizens in Massachusetts, New
York, or Illinois. Such inequality can not long
continue, but, if its long continuance were possible,
it would work the destruction of the Government
itself. The issue, then, is a vital one ; and, if the
ultimate result be not uncertain, then the more important it is to bring the contest to a close speedily.
Delay gives birth to hopes that must perish, embit-
ters the contestants, and checks or paralyzes private and public prosperity.

There is not a citizen of the North who is free
from responsibility or beyond the reach of this evil.
It touches with its malignant hand the humblest
laborer and the wealthiest capitalist. The laborer
of the South is driven in poverty from his home,
and the laborer of the North is cursed with an un-
natural and unhealthy competition. Capital loaned
or used in the South is without security. It finds
no protection either in local justice or in public
faith. By the force of events the laboring popula-

tion of the South is driven into the North, and by
the force of the same events the South is closed to
the labor and capital of the world. In many as-
pects the South is the chief sufferer. Even now it
approaches the admission that the abolition of
slavery was a good, and in twenty years more it
will accept the truth that there was no way to
prosperity except through justice to the black
man.

As States multiply, as population increases, as
representative constituencies are enlarged, the
power of the individual voter and of the State
diminishes. When the population of the Union
was but three million and the States were but
thirteen, the voice of Massachusetts in the Senate
was as two to twenty-six. In less than a hundred
years, two thirds of her power, speaking relatively
and numerically, have disappeared. Her vote in
the Senate is now only two in seventy-six, or one in
thirty-eight.

During the same period, however, the means of
communication and of influence have increased
even more rapidly than has been the increase of
population. Maine and California are nearer to
each other than were New Hampshire and Pennsylvania a hundred years ago; and there are now
no States so distant from the capital of the country
as were South Carolina and Georgia when the

15

Union was formed. The articles of " The Federalist " were delayed through successive weeks before they reached impatient readers in distant parts
of the country, while now the news of the morning,
the market, the courts, the Congress, is furnished
with equal accuracy and fullness in Washington, in
Maine, in Texas, in California, and in Oregon. If
the power of the individual ballot is less than it
once was, the idea behind the ballot has gained a
hundred-fold in opportunity for development and
influence.

We are now, therefore, more concerned about
the idea which directs the ballot than we are about
the name, residence, or race of the voter. All
opinions and all politics have become local, and all
opinions and all politics have become national.
Political outrages in Maine, Louisiana, and South
Carolina disturb and endanger the political rights
of men in every voting precinct and school district of the Union. The sovereignty of the States
is not disputed seriously ; the supremacy, the necessary, the inevitable, the constitutional supremacy
of the nation is everywhere more and more recognized ; but there are communities which deny to
the General Government the power to protect a
citizen of the United States in his political rights
against domestic violence, and yet have no scruples
about invoking the aid of the Union against yellow

fever imported from Havana, or pleuro-pneumonia threatened from Holland or Liverpool.

We are engaged in warm debate over an ancient tradition, whose origin is uncertain and whose value is doubtful; we vex the public ear with discussions touching appointments to office, the dangers of executive patronage, the power of office-holders, the duties on quinine and steel; and yield a quiet submission to the rule of a Senate and House of Representatives whose majorities were secured by the grossest usurpations, made possible only by the perpetration of the bloodiest of crimes.

In fine, public attention and the powers of Government are directed to topics of minor and temporary importance, while the real peril to which the country is exposed is either denied, or its consideration is avoided, or its importance is dwarfed.

If any words of mine can have value in the contest now opening, those words must relate to the issue I thus foreshadow.

The questions which I now treat as relatively unimportant would be worthy of earnest public consideration in ordinary times; but the grave question—the gravest of all questions—now is, *Shall this Government be destroyed or subverted permanently by the usurpations of a minority?*

It may be unpleasant to revive recollections of the war, but the war itself is intimately connected with recent events which have all the ear-marks of a powerful and continuing conspiracy. By the prosecution of the war, or as resulting from its successful issue, the Union was saved, slavery was destroyed, the blacks were enfranchised, the representative power of the old slave States was increased, and all by the efforts and concessions of the Republican party. More than this: By the magnanimity of the same party the authors and leaders of the rebellion were not only relieved from the punishment, and the peril of punishment, due to their crimes, but they were restored to their temporal possessions, and, with few exceptions, to all their political rights. How has this magnanimity been repaid? By the seizure of State after State through bloody scenes of crime and by criminal processes of fraud. Arkansas, Alabama, Louisiana, Mississippi, and South Carolina have been subjugated to the Democratic party, by the perpetration of the basest of crimes. Power thus acquired in those States is perpetuated in the hands of an armed minority by the continual practice of frauds which the majority, intimidated by the recollection of the bloody past, dare not either resist or expose. The conspirators, encouraged by their successes in the old slave States, and warned by the accumulating evidences of an adverse public sentiment in the North, sought, in their desperation, to render their supremacy absolute by the fraudulent seizure of the always free and intelligent State of Maine. There they have met their first defeat, but the processes employed connect the conspiracy in Maine and the conspiracy of the South with as much certainty as we connect the drifting icebergs of the Atlantic with the frozen seas of the North.

The patriotic men of the country are thus brought face to face with a great conspiracy which embraces the entire republic within the theatre of its operations. The central force of that conspiracy is the old slave power. Its purpose is to subjugate the Government to the ideas and policy of the slaveholding class. The chief means by which this policy can be made successful is the entire suppression of the negro vote in the fifteen old slave States. For the time this has been accomplished, and the result is seen in a Democratic Senate and a Democratic House of Representatives. Shall the presidency also be filled by a Democrat, and by the same means?

This conspiracy is within the Democratic party, and the Democratic party is its ally. It is, therefore, quite unimportant to inquire whether the conspiracy embrace the entire party or not; it is enough that the party is subservient to the conspiracy. The conspiracy triumphs when the party succeeds. The volumes of testimony taken in

Louisiana, Mississippi, North Carolina, Georgia, Alabama, and South Carolina prove the existence of the conspiracy. They prove, also, that its agents were sometimes White-Leaguers, sometimes Ku-klux, and sometimes Regulators, but that their acts and policy were always the same. As the conspiracy operates within and gives direction to the Democratic party, it is manifest that the Republican party is the only political organization which has either the disposition or the ability to change the course of events. And it must be admitted that the Republican party enters the contest defying a conspiracy which is already triumphant in the South. Of the fifteen old slave States it has usurped power in six, and suppressed freedom of political action in all the rest. A free vote and an honest count would insure the election of a Republican President and majorities in the Senate and House of Representatives. This vote can not be had, and the Republican party of the North is thereby deprived of the aid of its natural and trustworthy allies in the South. The conspiracy has made the South a unit, and the sole reliance of the Republican party is upon the North. In this exigency that party must nominate a candidate who can command an election, and who, when elected, will possess ability and courage to meet and master the difficulties that are sure to confront him. As it was certain in 1860 that the controlling force in the Democratic party contemplated rebellion, so now in 1880, it is as certain that the controlling force in the Democratic party contemplates the inauguration of the candidate of that party, whether he is or is not duly elected. The gravity of this contest can not be exaggerated. We know beforehand that the election of the Democratic candidate by honest means is an impossibility ; and yet the declaration of his election by the House and the Senate can be averted only by a victory on the part of the Republicans so decisive as to leave no ground for criticism or claim. Such claim is least likely to be made when the Republican party is under the lead of General Grant. General Grant is a man of peace ; but his capacity and firmness in defense of the rights and liberties of his country have been so often tested in great exigencies, that no further evidence is required either by friends or enemies.

If it be conceded that the States of the South, where the conspirators have usurped the governments and suppressed the ballot, are to be counted for the Democratic candidate, then the entire burden of the contest is thrown upon the State of New York. Without New York the Republican party can not succeed ; with New York the Republican party is sure of success.

The State of New York, in its position, in its

population, in its intelligence, in its industries, in its wealth, is the representative American State. The Republicans of that State, appreciating the solemnity of the crisis and the importance of their position, have declared their purpose to support General Grant for the presidency.

This purpose has not been formed hastily, nor has the expression of it been secured by extraordinary means. Something may be due to leadership, but men in masses do not change their opinions at the dictation of leaders. I place Mr. Conkling among the first of American statesmen, but I should do great injustice to his constituents if I asserted or admitted that they advocate or accept the nomination of General Grant under the influence of his lead. Indeed, not only in New York, but throughout the entire North, the voters, the rank and file of the party, as they are often designated, are more uniformly in favor of General Grant than are the leaders.

They feel, they know, indeed, that every important public interest will be safe in his hands. If the industry of the country can be promoted, he is its friend. If the public credit is assailed, he will stand in its defense. If a dishonest financial policy is proposed, he will not hesitate to resist it. If the lawful authority of the national Government is disputed, he will marshal and use all the resources of

that Government for the maintenance of that authority. And if the constitutional rights of citizens are invaded, he will employ every constitutional power for their protection. No doubt other
persons proposed as candidates might act in these
matters precisely as General Grant would act, but
there is no one of them all who can command as
great a following. Beyond all others, he represents the military spirit and the patriotic sentiment
of the country. Almost to the exclusion of every
other, his name is known and revered by the colored men of the South. It may not be possible to
redeem a single State from the domination of military rule, but something will be gained if the vic-
tims of the usurpation are led to make one serious
effort more in defense of their rights. On the
other hand, the violators of law in the South fear
General Grant more than they fear any one else.
To them he is the representative of that power by
which the rebellion was overthrown, the Union re-
established, and slavery abolished. His mastery
over great difficulties in the past has taught them
the important lesson that he will confront with confidence such difficulties as may arise in the future.

To the friends of law and order the nomination
of General Grant is the best security that can now
be had for peace and quiet ; to the enemies of law
and order his nomination means the exercise of

power and the administration of justice. Of this they may be assured.

Most men who have been advanced to places of honor and trust have been charged with ambition. General Grant has not escaped the charge. The ambition to acquire the faculty of honorably serving the public is a virtue; the ambition to rise to power by the overthrow of the public liberties is a crime. General Grant may fairly claim the virtue, and the suggestion that the crime can be laid at his door is but the grossest calumny. In a public experience of nearly forty years I have known something of public men, and among them all I can not recall one who gave more careful attention to every subject within the sphere of his duty.

It may not be possible for any man to give such assurances of fidelity to his country as to disarm criticism and suppress the spirit of malignity. General Grant has done all that it was possible for him to do, and no one has done more. He entered the service early in the war, and without regard to rank or position. He was never advanced upon his own solicitation. He gave everything he had, including the hazard of his life, to the service of his country. He was placed at the head of our armies by President Lincoln, and at the head of our armies he brought the war to a conclusion. When the hour of victory came he was the trusted leader of a million enthusiastic, trained, veteran warriors, and first of all he suggested and earnestly urged the disbandment of this immense force, and their speedy return to the arts and pursuits of peace. Now, in private life, crowned with every honor which his own or other lands can confer, he neither seeks nor shuns further public service. In the contest going on he takes no part. If by the unsolicited votes of his countrymen he is again called to the presidency, there ought not to be even one citizen base enough to suggest that he is animated by any purpose inconsistent with the constitutional requirements of the office.

This article is already burdened with the personality of the writer, but, as the evil can not now be remedied, I venture to increase it.

My relations to General Grant are those of sincere friendship; but, aside from that friendship, I recognize no personal obligation binding me to him. When he tendered me a place in his Cabinet, I declined it definitively; and it was only when, in peculiar circumstances, a further refusal seemed wholly inconsistent with my duty as a citizen and as a supporter of the Administration, that I accepted office. My position was an independent one, and I can now pass judgment upon General Grant with entire freedom. Pending the election in November last, I spoke at Bunker Hill; and what I then said concerning General Grant I now repeat:

"For the first time since General Grant left the office of President, I speak his name in public, and I do so now because I notice that many persons, from whom I did not expect so early a recognition of his character and services, have announced that they are disposed to support him for the presidency in 1880, or indicated the opinion that they expect his nomination and election. I may say, without assuming anything, that I have enjoyed the friendship of General Grant for many years, and I am not anxious that he should be again President of the United States. But I foresee that he is likely to be President. I do not know that the purpose to elect him is universal, but it appears to be very strong among the members of the Republican party, and I am disposed to see why it is that they look to General Grant. The instincts of great bodies of men usually have some good foundation, especially when the public sentiment runs for a long time in one direction, and there is no apparent moving force to the current. General Grant has been around the world. He has been in all the principal countries of Europe and of Asia, and if in those countries severally there has been one person, the ruler perhaps, who has been estimated as a more important personage than General

Grant, it appears to be but a repetition of what occurred in Greece when a vote was taken among
the commanders upon the question who was first
and who was second. Each officer voted for himself first, and Themistocles second. If you consider General Grant's career, it is not too much to
say that, in a military point of view, he is among
the first six men of whom history has preserved
any account; and if in future ages there shall be
those who claim for him the first place, it will not
be an extraordinary thing. Do you consider that
he commanded more men for a period of fifteen
months than were ever under the command of any
other general in ancient or modern times since the
days of Xerxes? That the theatre of his operations was as large as the entire scope of Napoleon's
campaigns from Egypt to Russia? That he never
received a suggestion or an order from a superior
in office after he became Lieutenant-General of the
Army? That he never held a council of war?
That he conducted operations at the same time up
and down the Mississippi River, across the continent, along the coast from Annapolis to Galveston,
and penetrated the Confederacy at two or three
points at the same time? That never, never in the
field, where he was in command personally, were
the troops under his orders routed, though they
were often shattered and afflicted by the severities

of the enemy's attacks? That they were never disheartened, discouraged, or demoralized, and that he brought to a successful conclusion the greatest war of modern times? Is it strange, then, that in all countries, even when stripped of the dignities of office and the formalities of power, he everywhere has been recognized as the first personage on the surface of the earth? Under these circumstances, is it strange that the Republican party of this country turns to him? I have said this of General Grant, not because I want him nominated for the presidency. I think it has responsibilities from which he may well shrink. I do not know that an election will add to his fame. I am sure it will not increase his happiness. But there have been times when even in Massachusetts, and in Republican assemblies, it was not easy to represent General Grant as he is—a man of imperturbable spirit, full of patriotism, animated by a plain and loving sense of justice, and anxious— more anxious, perhaps, than any other American citizen—for the perpetuity of our institutions, for the preservation of our national honor, and for the glory and prosperity of his country."

THE END.

BIOGRAPHY.

THE HUNDRED GREATEST MEN. PORTRAITS OF THE ONE HUNDRED GREATEST MEN OF HISTORY. Reproduced from Fine and Rare Steel Engravings, with Biographies. 8vo. Cloth, $6.00.

A General Introduction to the Work was written by RALPH WALDO EMERSON; Introduction to Section I by MATTHEW ARNOLD; Section II by H. TAINE; Section III by MAX MÜLLER and R. RENAN; Section IV by NOAH PORTER; Section V by A. P. STANLEY; Section VI by H. HELMHOLTZ; Section VII by J. A. FROUDE; Section VIII by Professor JOHN FISKE.

HOURS WITH GREEK AND LATIN AUTHORS. From Various English Translations. With Biographical Notices. By G. H. JENNINGS and W. S. JOHNSTONE. 12mo. Cloth, $2.00.

LIFE OF HIS ROYAL HIGHNESS THE PRINCE CONSORT. By Sir THEODORE MARTIN. With Portraits and Views. Complete in 5 vols. 12mo. Cloth, $10.00.

"The literature of England is richer by a book which will be read with profit by succeeding generations of her sons and daughters."—*Blackwood.*

BEACONSFIELD. A SKETCH OF THE LITERARY AND POLITICAL CAREER OF BENJAMIN DISRAELI (Earl of Beaconsfield). With Two Portraits. By GEORGE M. TOWLE. 18mo. Paper, 25 cents; cloth, 60 cents.

LIFE OF CHARLOTTE BRONTE. By E. C. GASKELL. With Engravings. Two volumes in one. 12mo. Cloth, $1.50.

Charlotte Brontë was one of the most extraordinary female characters of modern times. From perfect obscurity, and notwithstanding a most unpropitious training, she sprang at once bound to the height of popularity, founded an entirely new school of novel-writing, and, after a life of severe trial and suffering, died when she was just beginning to be happy.

LIFE AND WRITINGS OF THOMAS HENRY BUCKLE. By ALFRED HENRY HUTH. 12mo. Cloth, $2.00.

"The book deals with Mr. Buckle less as a philosopher than as a man. . . . Mr. Huth has done his part well and thoroughly."—*Saturday Review.*

THOMAS CARLYLE: HIS LIFE—HIS BOOKS—HIS THEORIES. By ALFRED H. GUERNSEY. 18mo. Paper, 30 cents; Cloth, 60 cents.

New York: D. APPLETON & CO., 1, 3, & 5 Bond Street.

BIOGRAPHY.

ERASMUS DARWIN. By Ernst Kraus. Translated from the German by W. S. Dallas. With a Preliminary Notice by Charles Darwin. With Portraits and Woodcuts. 12mo. Cloth, $1.25.

CHARLES DARWIN. By Grant Allen. (English Worthies Series.) 16mo. Cloth, 75 cents.

LIFE OF CHARLES DICKENS. By John Forster. The concluding volume of Chapman & Hall's Household Edition of the Works of Charles Dickens. With 40 Illustrations. Square 8vo. Paper, $1.25; cloth, $1.75.

SHORT LIFE OF CHARLES DICKENS. With Selections from his Letters. By Charles H. Jones. 18mo. Paper, 35 cents; cloth, 60 cents.

FARADAY AS A DISCOVERER. A Memoir. By Professor John Tyndall. 12mo. Cloth, $1.00.

"It has been thought desirable to give you and the world some image of Michael Faraday as a scientific investigator and discoverer. . . . I have returned from my task with such results as I could gather, and also with the wish that these results were more worthy than they are of the greatness of my theme."—*The Author.*

SHORT LIFE OF GLADSTONE. By C. H. Jones. 18mo. Paper, 35 cents; cloth, 60 cents.

"In two hundred and fifty pages, the author has succeeded in giving a clear impression of Gladstone's career, and, what is better still, of his personality. Extracts from his speeches and estimates of his literary work are given, and an excellent feature of the book is its short but significant citations from the press, which help the reader to see the great statesman through the eyes of his contemporaries, both friend and foe."—*Boston Courier.*

A JOURNAL OF THE REIGNS OF KING GEORGE IV AND KING WILLIAM IV. By the late Charles C. F. Greville, Esq., Clerk of the Council to those Sovereigns. Edited by Henry Reeve, Registrar of the Privy Council. 2 vols. 12mo. Cloth, $4.00.

"Since the publication of Horace Walpole's Letters, no book of greater historical interest has seen the light than the Greville Memoirs. It throws a curious, and, we may almost say, a terrible light on the conduct and character of the public men in England under the reigns of George IV and William IV. Its descriptions of those kings and their kinsfolk are never likely to be forgotten."—*New York Times.*

New York: D. APPLETON & CO., 1, 3, & 5 Bond Street.

www.ingramcontent.com/pod-product-compliance
Lightning Source LLC
Chambersburg PA
CBHW020115030726
47498CB00006B/2119